CLAW

CATNIP ASSASSINS BOOK 6

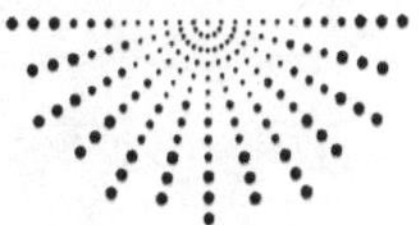

SKYE MACKINNON

Peryton Press

BLURB

They took her freedom. Now she'll take their lives.

Voluntary kidnapping. That's new even for Kat. Trapped, tortured and without any sign of her sister's whereabouts, she can only do one thing: release the beast within and hope she doesn't lose her humanity. Nor her family.

Relationships will be broken. New alliances will be forged. And yes, there will be more kittens.

The sixth book in this purrfectly exciting urban fantasy series full of action, suspense and cat puns. A slow burn reverse harem where Kat won't have to choose.

A QUICK WORD BEFORE WE GET STARTED

As you will know from the previous three books, this series is set in a world very similar to our own, but there are some deciding differences. Technology has developed differently, and while there are many devices you may be used to, such as televisions, there are no mobile phones, cars or the internet. No guns, either.

$$* * * * * *$$

This book is written in British English and uses some British expressions and idioms. Please don't see these as spelling mistakes. We say mum rather than mom, use a lot of 's' instead of 'z' (cosy, realise, …) and use 'got' as the past participle of 'get' (instead of 'gotten').

$$* * * * * *$$

And finally, subscribe to Skye's newsletter for updates about new releases: skyemackinnon.com/newsletter.

You'll even get a free book for subscribing, so it's totally worth it.

WHAT HAPPENED BEFORE

In Lick, the fifth book in the series, Kat and her family packed up their bags and moved to Attenburgh, ready to start a new life. Before she's properly settled, she gets a mysterious letter offering her the 'business opportunity of the century'. Obviously, she can't resist and is soon in the middle of a treasure hunt that brings her employees into danger.

At the same time, she starts working for the mayor of Attenburgh, Lady Lara, a woman both beautiful and intelligent. While her job is supposed to be protecting the mayor, it's actually Kat who gets attacked and almost killed by a siren.

In the middle of trying to find out who's out to kill her, Kat and her friends manage to steal a diamond at a Jewellers' Guild Ball (despite some potentially deadly traps), but Kat isn't very happy when she finds out who gave them the mysterious task: the mayor herself. Lady Lara was out to purge the city of the most successful thieves and assassins, but never intended to harm Kat.

Grudgingly, Kat agrees to work as the mayor's advisor

and help her use different methods to stop the evil sirens using Attenburgh's underworld to do their bidding. Before she can start her new job though, a siren appears at her doorstep with Kat's missing sister/clone, K7. He gives her a choice: he'll kill her sister unless she becomes his captive. Of course, Kat chooses to save her sister and steps into the cage the siren brought for her.

CHAPTER ONE

Being kidnapped is no fun at all. Being tortured is even more tedious.

I've lost all track of time. Has it been weeks? Months? My cell doesn't have a window and the flickering light on the ceiling stays on every hour of the day. In the beginning, I tried to keep count of days, but I quickly lost all interest in that. What does it matter how long I've been kept prisoner? All I should focus on is getting out of here.

Which is easier said than done. The cell door has no lock I could pick with my claws. There is no window to climb out of. My food and water are delivered through a pipe to the right of the door. It's wide enough for me to stick my arm in, but it's no means of escape.

I get food at random intervals. Sometimes they keep me waiting for what feels like ten hours, sometimes I get a new delivery through the pipe while I'm still eating the last meal. I bet they do it on purpose to make it harder for me to adjust to a routine.

Eating is my only entertainment. I've not spoken to anyone since I was voluntarily kidnapped. I don't know if they keep my sister in the same building. I don't even know if the siren is here. He's not come to visit. He was probably watching me through the camera on the ceiling until I covered it in my own shit. It was the only sticky material I had access to.

Instead of a toilet, they've given me a potty. Luckily, it's adult size. The container beneath is lined with a bag, and when the bag is full, I knot it close and squeeze it into the pipe. It then gets sucked out just before my next meal is delivered. It's a yucky way of doing things, but I've got used to it. What I really miss is a shower. I wash myself with the water I get with my food, but no matter how clean I try to keep myself and my clothes, I've started to smell rank. I wouldn't want to be in my own company, but sadly I'm forced to be.

And all this time, not a single word from anyone. No guards move outside my door. The pipe is my only contact to the outside world. I've shouted into it, hoping it might be connected to other cells, but no luck. For all I know, I'm the only prisoner here.

I'm not sure what the walls are made of or how thick they are, but no sound filters through them. Even with my cat senses, I have no idea what's going on around me.

Basically, I'm bored as fuck. My meal delivery has become the highlight of my day. I savour every bite of the surprisingly good food, trying to distinguish between the ingredients. It's my game. Sadly, I have no idea if I ever get the correct answer. There's no one to ask what they put into my food. Today – or it could have been yesterday – I got raisin dumplings along with two bottles of water. I used one of them to wash my hair. It's a matted mess that resembles a bird's nest built by a very inexperienced bird. I may have to cut it off once I get out of here.

It's not if. It's when.

I'm not giving up. My team is out there. My family. I doubt they'll just forget about me and move on. They'll be looking for me. Annoyingly, I don't even know if I'm still in Attenburgh. They drugged me as soon as I entered the cage.

I could be back home. Or I could be in an entirely different city. There's no way to know. Luckily, all my men are excellent trackers. Lennox especially with his wolf senses.

Still, I can't rely on them to rescue me. I'm my own woman. If there is a way out of here, I will find it. When they finally open my door.

They have found a way to torture me without ever entering my cell. It's kind of ingenious, if I may say so myself. Loud music that threatens to make my eardrums explode. The floor turning scalding hot while I'm sitting down. It's why I always stay close to my cot now. Burns heal slowly even with my shifter healing abilities. The worst is the fog though. It comes every few days and fills my cell until I can't help but breathe it in. It burns my lungs, steals my strength, gives me the most terrifying hallucinations. The worst is that there's nothing I can do to stop it. I can't fight an enemy who's not in the same room with me.

I sigh and take a swig out of my water bottle. I swirl the liquid around my mouth, moving it in a perfect circle. Yet another one of my new hobbies. There are only so many activities you can do in a room with nothing but a potty and a bed. I glare at the cot. The bedding is the same as when I arrived here and it's smelly as hell. No wonder, since I'm smelly too. I've tried sleeping without the blanket, but it gets cold in here. Some nights - or days, who knows - I shift to sleep, but that is getting ever harder. Without the chance to move and run, my cat is restless. I'm close to losing control of her every time I shift. I've seen shifters whose animal sides have turned crazy. It's not a pretty sight. So I stay human as much as I can, biding my time. Once the door opens, I'll shift and tear apart anyone who stands in my way. They'll regret locking me up. Not that I'll give them much time to feel regret before I'll rip out their throats.

I lick my lips. It's going to be very satisfying. I miss the smell of blood. And the taste.

No, that's wrong. I don't want to fall victim to those cravings again. Killing is good. Enjoying my victims' blood isn't. I'm an assassin, not a serial killer. There's a difference. Yes, it's a fine line, but the line exists. Lennox and I had a long discussion about that once before he escaped the Pack. I smile at the memory. It was after his first kill. He was a gentle boy back then, someone who would never have hurt anyone if he hadn't been forced to do so. The Pack turned him into a killer. There's not much left of that innocent boy who decided he was going to be an assassin rather than a murderer. I wonder if he still feels remorse when he kills, or if it's become his normality.

I've always been different. I enjoy the hunt, the adrenaline, the kill. The moment the life flickers out in my victim's eyes. Extinguishing the spark of life is one of the most exhilarating feelings in the world. Only good sex comes anywhere close.

Not that I'd ever kill without reason. I'm not a monster. It's my profession to assassinate, and I enjoy it. Killing someone who deserves it is far more enjoyable than randomly murdering someone. I think it's thanks to Lennox that I don't overstep that line. He's made me a better person without even knowing.

My heart clenches at the thought of him. And of the others. Gryphon. Ryker. My sisters. Bethany, Lily and Benjamin. They're all my family. Growing up, I always tried not to get attached. The pain of losing Lennox had been too much. I'd built stone walls around my heart after he left, unwilling to ever feel that kind of pain again. Maybe it was a mistake to let them crush my walls and let them into my heart. Is the happiness I feel when being around them worth the agony of missing them?

I'm not sure. Sometimes I wake up on a pillow wet with tears. I bet if I shook my pillow a couple of times, I'd get enough salt from it for an entire saltshaker. I rarely remember my dreams, but I assume they're about my family.

I drink the last of my water and stick the empty bottle into the pipe. It will be sucked in whenever they decide to bring me my next meal. I'm already looking forward to it. Not because I'm hungry, but because I'm bored.

In the past, I cut up the water bottles with my claws to make improvised knives and later art. Not that I'm a very arty person, but boredom is bringing out strange sides to me that I didn't know existed.

I later destroyed my plastic sculptures in a fit of rage. I guess that's good. In case I'm rescued soon, I don't want to leave any evidence of my newfound creative skills. It wouldn't fit the no-nonsense persona I've painstakingly built over the years. There's never been room in my life for useless hobbies such as art, and that won't change. Even though I kind of liked my sculptures.

I pull my blanket around my shoulders and curl up on the bed, trying not to breathe in through my nose. It's hard to relax when you smell your own rancid odour. If it weren't so cold in this cell, I'd stuff the blanket in the pipe. Maybe I should try it nonetheless. They might give me a new one. But I'm not sure I want to risk it. I laugh darkly. Look at me, suddenly afraid to take risks. That's so not like me. Risktaker is my middle name.

Being in this cell is breaking me. It's a slow process, but I know it's happening. There's nothing I can do about it. I can't escape without someone opening the door. All I can try to do is keep a hold on my sanity.

One day, that door will have to open.

CHAPTER TWO

I stare at myself in the mirror. My hair hangs in dirty streaks, hiding most of my face. I pull one strand back and tuck it behind my ear, exposing my right eye. I gasp.

No, I don't. Well, I do, mentally, but the girl in the mirror doesn't. She just stares at her reflection.

She's not me.

I'm not her.

My thoughts are sluggish and it takes me far too long to realise who she is. My sister. K7. I'm looking through her eyes. Is this a dream? It has to be.

I take the opportunity to look at her, take her in. Back when I saw her with the siren, I didn't have the time to properly look at my sister. I recognised her, but that was about it.

Obviously, the first thing that stands out is her right eye. It's bright silver, almost metallic. I've never seen anything like it. It's natural, I think, not some kind of technology implant, but it's still a little creepy. The rest of her face - at least the parts that peek out from behind her wild mane - is how I remember myself looking at her age. Her lips are pressed tightly together, but that's the only sign of any *emotion she might feel. Her face is blank, especially her eyes. It creeps me out. Despite everything that was done to me, I never looked like that. I never gave up. I fought, I rebelled, I got punished, but I always got back up and continued to fight even harder. It's different for her. Little K7. She's dead inside and I think she knows it.*

She keeps staring into the mirror. I'd love to turn away, but I'm trapped, unable to stop looking through her eyes. Please let me wake up from this nightmare. Now.

She blinks and I realise she's not done that the entire time I've been inside of her. Creepy. It's what they say about psychopaths, right? That they don't blink as often as normal people. But this has been several minutes. I don't know what's wrong with my sister, but I bet it's a lot. Who knows what they've done to her since she was created. She's not wearing a collar, which scares me the most. She's still here, she's not run away, which must mean she's completely under their control with no need for a collar. I really don't want to doubt my ability to save her, but I'm starting to. She might be too far gone. But no, I couldn't leave her behind. There's no chance of that. When I escape, she's coming with me and I'm going to find a way to turn her into the happy child she should be. Both Caitlin and K8 are more or less rehabilitated. I'm sure it can be done again.

With another blink, she turns away from the mirror, giving me a view of the room we're in. It's a small bedroom, with a single bed, a wardrobe and a table and chair, but what really draws my eye is the screen on the wall. I would have staggered back if I'd been in my own body. Then I would have covered my eyes and tried to forget.

But I can't. There's nothing I can do but stare at myself, in the white room, screaming because of the searing hot floor. And the worst thing is that I feel K7 smile.

❀ ❀ ❀ ❀ ❀ ❀

IT MUST HAVE BEEN MONTHS. I HAVE LOST ALL TRACK OF time, but it feels like many, many weeks have passed. Eat, torture, sleep, repeat. I've settled into a routine, dragging myself from day to day. The only thing that keeps me going is the thought of my family. They're out there, somewhere. I have something to live for. I need to keep going.

The first sign something new is about to happen is the lights flashing brighter. I squeeze my eyes shut as my room is suddenly drenched in something akin to sunlight on a summer's day. No more dim, flickering light. I always assumed the bulb was faulty, but it seems that was yet another way of them to annoy me.

I get to my feet, trying to stand as tall as I can without wobbling. The food rations have decreased recently and I'm constantly feeling light-headed. If their intention is to starve me, they're doing an excellent job. My plan had always been to shift as soon as the door opens, but I doubt I'd have the strength to do that now. If I shift, I might get stuck in between shapes, and that could end up killing me. No, I'm going to have to stay human and just hope that I'll be able to get out of here without my cat's additional strength.

Footsteps approach from afar, echoing in what must be a narrow corridor outside my cell. It's the first time in months that I've heard another person. I always thought I'd do well as a hermit, but to be honest, I'm looking forward to seeing someone else, even if it's an enemy. Now the question is, wait and see what's happening, or attack and run? A few weeks ago, I'd done the latter without question, but I've grown too weak. I don't know how long I could run without collapsing. I grit my teeth in frustration. I've turned from a strong, successful assassin into a pitiful prisoner, too feeble to escape her goalers. It makes me want to cry and scream. And then kill those who've done this to me.

I step back until my back hits the cold wall behind me. It helps with making it appear as if I'm strong enough to stand up straight. Which I'm not. My legs are threatening to give way beneath me. The starvation has got me almost exactly where they want me to be. Crawling on the floor. I'm not going to give them that satisfaction. I'd rather die trying to escape. No more torture. *No more.*

"No more."

I say it out loud. My voice is hoarse from misuse, but I say it again and again until the words are audible.

"No more."

The footsteps stop outside and the door opens in slow motion. Hurry up. My vision is turning black at the edges. I won't be able to stay upright for much longer.

A woman steps into the room. Not someone I've seen before. She's nothing special, absolutely ordinary. Her face would be pretty if her eyes weren't as far apart. Her clothes are good quality but wouldn't make her stand out in a crowd. She smells faintly of siren. It's either in her heritage or she's been close to one recently. I guess the latter, if this is my kidnapper's wife.

Behind her are two large men. I sniff the air. They're mutants, the creatures I've fought before. My mouth waters. I remember how good their blood tasted. How it made me feel stronger. If I get to drink their blood, I might regain enough strength to get out of here. The woman must think they're her protection. In fact, they could be my salvation.

"You look pathetic," she says coldly as if we already know each other.

"So do you. Scared to be on your own with me?"

Her expression doesn't change at all. "Not scared. Wise. I know what you are and what you can do. I'm not a foolish woman, no matter what my husband may think."

I wonder if her husband is the man who kidnapped me.

"You look remarkably similar," she says, studying me from top to toe. "I guess I know now what my baby will look like when she's all grown up."

Her baby? K7, maybe? Or another, younger clone? I surely hope not. Once I've rescued K7 - and I will rescue her, no doubt about that - all of us are accounted for. No more searching for my lost sisters. I'll be able to settle down and go back to killing people for money. The simple life. Oh, how I miss it.

"My daughter has been looking forward to meeting you," the woman continued. "She got so excited when my husband finally captured you. It's been hard keeping her from visiting you, but she understands that you're not quite ready to see her yet."

"Not ready?" I ask. I'm so confused. My brain feels too weak to think.

"You're not ready to listen. If I told you why you're here just now, you'd not accept the truth. You're not ready."

I grin at her. I bet I look completely crazed. "Go ahead, tell me all your evil plans. I'll listen."

Her expression doesn't change. "As I said. You're not ready. Maybe in a couple of weeks. Until then, I'll have to find ways to keep my baby busy, to distract her from wanting to see you. She's desperate for a playmate, especially one who looks like her."

"Feel free to let her visit me. I'd love to get to know my sister."

The woman laughs coldly. "She's not your sister. She's so much better than you will ever be."

And with that, she leaves, taking her goons with her. I stay standing for a few more seconds, just in case she returns, before letting myself drop to the floor. My muscles ache from standing for so long. I'm not used to it anymore. Urgh. I hate the state I'm in. I can't even stand for longer than a few minutes. What kind of wreck have I become?

⁂

THE DAYS PASS SLOWLY. THEY GIVE ME BARELY ANY FOOD. I get even weaker. And the torture continues. The floor grows so hot I have burns all over my body. They heal almost as slow as if I were human. And all the while, I wonder if K7 is watching me. It could have been a dream, but after meeting that woman, I'm pretty sure it was real. Something strange is going on here, with her and my sister, and I need to find out what it is so I can escape and take K7 with me. I want her to be safe, even now, even after seeing her smiling at me being tortured. She can't help how she was raised. Who knows what they did to her.

I spend my time counting how often the light flickers. I count my own heartbeat. I picture my men and try to remember what they smelled like. It's getting harder to hold on to those memories. Sometimes, just when I think I can see them in front of my inner eye, they dissolve and the memory slips from my grasp. I'm not a crier, but I can't help the tears in those moments. I'm losing my hold on the people that keep me going and that scares me shitless. If I can't picture them anymore, what will I have left to fight for?

Loneliness plays tricks with my mind. From time to time, I hear meows, so clear as if a cat is inside my cell but, of course, there isn't. I think it's just an auditory hallucination.

I curl up and cover my eyes with my hands to keep the

flashing light from irritating me. It's driving me crazy. Everything is. I'm slipping into madness and nothing is stopping me from losing my grasp on reality.

CHAPTER THREE

I wake up in an unfamiliar room. It's not my cell. I blink to clear my vision, unable to believe what I'm seeing. The four-poster bed, the plush carpets, the heavy curtains, the heavy walnut furniture. I'm in a giant room that looks like it could be in a palace or manor house. Everything is luxurious and expensive.

Funnily enough, I feel more uncomfortable here than I did in my cell.

I sit up. Darkness creeps around the edges of my vision, but I manage not to faint. The mattress beneath me is soft, softer than anything I've touched in weeks. Or months; I wouldn't know. Time has become meaningless.

I'm wearing a sleeveless dress; simple linen but clean. I sniff myself. No, I'm not clean. They only changed my clothes.

I run my hands over the blanket covering me. Fluffy. Like fur. I close my eyes and imagine that this is Ryker's fur. His head on my lap, his tail tapping the floor like it always does when he's happy. His contented purr filling the room.

Slowly, I slide out of bed and extend my senses. Unlike

back in the cell, I can hear noises from all around me. People talking, moving around, animals in the distance. My senses are weakened, but probably still better than those humans are cursed with. I walk over to the door and close my eyes, focusing on the closest voices. A male and a female, whispering. I wonder if they're talking quietly because they're worried I may hear them, or if they don't want to be overheard by other people.

"It's a travesty," the woman whispers. "They didn't let me wash her. The sheets will be ruined."

"Who is she?" the man asks.

"She looks like the Little Mistress, just older. I wonder if they're related."

The man huffs. "Let's hope not. One brat is enough for me."

"Shush, someone might hear. You don't want to end up like Jack."

"I've applied for a job at Lord Lear's household. If I get it, I'll finally be away from all this craziness. I've had enough."

"Let me know if they have any other jobs going," the woman whispers. "The Little Mistress bit me again yesterday. Just look at the wound, it's like a wild animal ripped into my skin."

Silence, followed by the man gasping. "You shouldn't let her do that. What if the wound gets infected? It's bad enough that Jenny lost her hand. You don't want that to happen to you."

The woman huffs. "It's not as if I have a choice. That girl does what she wants and nobody dares to stop her. The lady even encourages her. She didn't blink an eyelid when I told her I'd been bitten. She didn't even give me time to clean the wound."

"I'll be sure to ask if Lord Lear has any other

vacancies," the man promises.

A shattering sound makes them both shut up; I think they broke a plate or something like that. I've heard enough though to build a picture. The staff here are unhappy. K7 bites people. And the lady of the house is just as cold as I judged her when she'd stepped into my cell. For now, none of that helps me escape, but it gives me hope. If the staff aren't loyal to their employers, I may be able to bribe them into helping me.

First though, I have to figure out why I'm in this room and no longer trapped. I walk over to the window and open the ruby red curtains. I almost laugh in disappointment. I expected there to be a window that may be my way out of here. But no. From the stone arch, it's clear that there used to be a window here, but it's been bricked up many years ago. The curtains are just for show. I glare at the stone wall and let the curtains fall back into their original place, hiding the traitorous non-window that gave me hope.

The only way out of the room seems to be the door, but I'm somewhat reluctant to try that. In the past, I would have simply unlocked the door - using lock picks if necessary - and ran out of here, killing anyone who stood in my way. Now, I can barely walk, let alone fight or run. And I bet my captors are very aware of that. They've waited for this moment where I'm no longer a physical threat to them. A kitten is more dangerous than me right now. I think of Pumpkin, Ryker's little son. I miss him. He'd scratch me for calling him little, but that only makes him cuter.

With a sigh, I put my hand on the round doorknob and twist. The door opens with a click. By the great cat gods.

They're really making it too easy. Or they're playing a game with me. Much more likely. I can't resist the temptation though.

I walk out of my room, using the walls to steady me. My vision keeps getting dark around the edges, but I ignore it. I'm not going to faint; I won't allow it. I walk past several closed doors before I reach the kitchen. There's no sign of the two people who were talking earlier, but a few porcelain shards on the floor lie witness to them having been here. I should find the exit, but my stomach growls at the smell of food. When did I last eat? It must be days. And I need water. I won't get far if I'm as weak as I am now.

I find a plate of made up sandwich fingers in the fridge and hungrily devour half of them, before stuffing the rest in a plastic bag I find in a drawer. The only bottle I find is a glass milk bottle, but that suits me fine. I drink with pure joy, savouring the taste of the cool milk. After so long of subsisting on nothing but water, dry bread and occasional porridge, this is like a bowl of catnip in heaven. In the beginning, they gave me good, proper food, but that changed pretty quickly. It's been long enough for something as simple as milk to cause an explosion of taste on my tongue.

Before I leave the kitchen, a knife block on the counter catches my eyes. Come to mummy, pretty babies. I wish my dress had pockets or a belt to stuff some knives in. Instead, I add two small knives to my plastic bag and hold the biggest one in my hand. Even with me being weak, I think I could still do some serious harm with a blade.

I've only just eaten, but I'm already feeling a little steadier on my feet. Maybe I'm imagining it, but it's not like it matters. Only results count. Never let your own feelings deceive you. Everybody lies, including your senses. The Pack teachings have never rung more true.

I leave the kitchen and sniff the air, looking for the smell of fresh air, maybe grass. The outside world. The scent is faint, as if I'm either far above or far below ground. That makes me realise that I've not seen a single window so far. All the light has been artificial. I try and remember the dream I had about K7. Yes, I think her small room had a window. That gives me hope. I'm sure she was in the same building. Light, here I come.

I round a corner. Two mutants are waiting for me. Before I can even throw my knife, something pricks my neck and I collapse, my body refusing to move. How didn't I hear them? Just before darkness takes me, I realise the cause. They have no heartbeats.

I WAKE IN THE SAME SOFT BED IN THE SAME EMPTY ROOM. I almost wish I was back in my cell. The routine of eat, sleep, torture, repeat has become familiar. This is new and I don't like it. My stomach aches with hunger. I must have been out cold for a while. I sit up and wait for the room to stop spinning.

This time, I don't check the window and go straight to the door. It's unlocked. They're toying with me. Still, I can't get myself to stay in this room. Just like before - yesterday? - I walk down the corridor, but this time I pass the kitchen, unwilling to waste any time. At the corner of the hallway where I was confronted by the two mutants, I stop and extend my senses. Nothing. No smells, no sounds. That alarms me in itself. A house should never be this quiet. I don't believe that nobody else is here. They'd not leave me on my own. No, this is their game that I'm playing without actually knowing the rules.

I somehow need to turn the tables. Do something they don't expect. There have to be more options than trying to escape and staying in that room. Right? They might also expect me to try and rescue K7, but there's no way I'd manage that in my current condition. No, I need to get out of here, recuperate, and then return with back up. It's not like she's in immediate danger. I shudder as the image of her smiling flashes through my mind. No, concentrate.

I could hide somewhere in the house and then try and sneak out later. But if K7 has anything like my own senses, she'd find me immediately. Not a risk I'm willing to take. If I were stronger, I might confront the lady of the house and the man who kidnapped me. Well, forced me to self-kidnap. Same thing. But that wouldn't end well. So what else can I do? I can't run, I can't stay, I can't fight. That doesn't leave a whole lot of options. The only thing left is getting help. How I hate it. I don't like depending on other people. Even if those people are cats.

I slip into a room to my left and lock the door. It's a bedroom that looks like it hasn't been used in months. A fine layer of dust coats the shaggy carpet. Perfect, nobody is going to come in here by accident. Again, there's nothing but a brick wall behind the curtains, but I have to hope that I'm not too far away from the outside world.

I take a deep breath, then whistle on the exhale. It's so high-pitched that humans won't be able to hear it, and unless K7 regularly communicates with cats, she wouldn't recognise it as the cry for help that it is. I'm calling for assistance. Let's hope the local cats use the same signal as the cats in Attenburgh and back home. I'm pretty sure they do; cat language is universal, except for some dialects. And for all I know, I could still be in Attenburgh. it's unlikely, but I can't discount the possibility.

Now all I can do is wait and hope that somecat heard my call. What I need next is food and weapons. Same as yesterday, really, but I don't want to go to that kitchen again. I can't do the same things as before, or they'll catch me even quicker. I ball my hands into fists. I can't give up. I need to fight the hopelessness that's threatening to take hold of me. If I give up hope, I'm as good as dead. You've got this, Kat. Think.

I turn and look around the room, desperate for inspiration. My eyes fall on the curtains. The fake window. If it was bricked up long ago, the mortar gluing the bricks together might have become brittle. It's a fool's hope, but I don't have any better ideas. I pull open the curtains and inspect the wall. With a fingernail, I scratch at the mortar. It dissolves into sand. That's a good sign.

After some rummaging in cupboards, I clutch my prize. A pair of knitting needles, discarded along with a ball of wool. Back before I was captured, I would have had to fight my inner cat at the sight of wool, but now, my cat is buried so deep that I couldn't care less. I doubt even catnip would do much for me now. Because I was worried I'd go feral, I pushed my cat away, locking it behind a thick barrier. It's hurting both the cat and my human side, but it can't be helped.

The sound of the needle scraping against brick is terribly loud to my ears, but I can't help it. I work as quietly as I can, pushing it in further and further. Sweat leaks from my pores. This isn't hard work, but my body isn't used to moving anymore. By the time the end of the needle breaks through the last bits of mortar, I'm ready to faint.

I pull it back and stare through the tiny hole. I'd hoped

for sunlight, but there's none of that. No light at all. Frowning, I push the needle in again and probe for whatever may be behind the wall. With a clonk, it hits something metal. Curious. I move the needle from left to right as much as I can, but there's nothing but metal. It sounds thick, like it's more than just a thin sheet. I wonder what this means. A secondary wall? If so, just on this side or surrounding the entire house?

It would explain the lack of noise and smells from the outside. It will also make escaping a whole lot harder.

I press my mouth against the hole and repeat my shrill cat call. Please, feline gods amongst the stars, let this work.

There's nothing left for me to do here. I hold the needles like knives and leave the room. This time, I'm even more alert, knowing that I can't trust my hearing. I still can't quite believe that those two grunts didn't have a heartbeat, but I'm clever enough to learn from the experience.

Before I round the corner where they caught me, I grab my needles even tighter and prepare to dive out of the way should they throw a poison dart at me again. But nobody is waiting for me. Either by luck or by design of their game; I don't know, I don't care. The corridor is short and leads to two doors. One of them must open to either an exit or yet another hallway, unless this house is a labyrinth. I wouldn't put it past them. I press an ear against both of them, but no suspicious sounds reach me. Alright, I chose a door to my left earlier, this time I'll go right.

It's another bedroom. How many people are they housing here? Again, it's been unused for a while though. I quickly check behind the curtains - yes, another fake window - and then try the second door. A staircase leading up. As good as anything, I suppose.

I tiptoe up the steps until I'm in front of yet another

door. This one is locked, but I now have my handy knitting needles. They're nowhere near as good as lock picks, but after several attempts, the lock clicks open. As quietly as I can, I pull open the door - and stare in the yellow eyes of a mutant. He grins wickedly and presses one hand against my chest. I stab him with one of my needles, but it's too late, I'm falling backwards, falling, crashing, tumbling.

Gone.

Everything hurts. My body is one big bruise. But I'm back in the four-poster bed with the soft mattress. This time, though, I'm naked. They've taken my clothes. Fuck them. That's not going to stop me. I was born naked, as was every single person in this world. Nakedness is a state of mind. You can either rule it or let it intimidate you.

I can't stop a groan as I sit up. Pain is everywhere. One of my ankles feels as if it's broken. No exploring for me today. Maybe it's time to wait for them to come to me and tell me what this is all about. It's ridiculous that I've been a prisoner here for months and still haven't got the faintest idea why. Yes, they probably love torturing me, but there's no point to it. They've not tried to get information from me. That's what torture is usually for, right? At least based on *my* training. And in all the years of being an assassin, I've never heard of anyone putting their prisoner into a fancy *unlocked* room. It doesn't make any sense at all. That worries me. If I don't know what my enemies are up to, it's much harder to predict their next move and how to counteract it.

If I knew they wanted me dead, I could always play dead and hope they carry my body out of this house. But I'm pretty sure they like me alive. Torture is much more entertaining with a living body.

I extend my senses to see if I can listen in on a servant conversation again. No such luck; the house is quiet.

My stomach growls at the same time as my bladder signals me that it's time to find a loo. That makes me realise that I've not used a toilet ever since I first woke up in this room. How weird. I guess it's either because I've not had enough fluids, or because they do something to me while I'm unconscious. Either way, I need a toilet.

I get up and curse as I try and put weight on my injured ankle. If it's not broken, then it's sprained at the very least. Just what I needed. Now I'm a sitting duck...cat. No, I'm nowhere near being a cat. I've lost my strength and spirit. They've broken most of me, as much as it pains me to admit that.

I limp out of the room, cursing at every step. My body is on fire with pain. Is that how humans feel after tumbling down a staircase? Being human must suck. I wish I had my healing abilities back, but they seem to be out of commission.

I dimly remember seeing a bathroom yesterday but ignoring it while walking past. It takes me ten painful minutes to find it again. It's a big room with a golden bathtub that sits on four lion's paws. Ridiculous. I lock the door behind me and pee to my heart's content. At least I still have control over my bladder. Small mercies.

Now that I'm here, I use the opportunity to look for escape routes from the bathroom. There's no window, obviously, but a grate above a towel stand catches my eye. Ventilation, I assume. It might be just big enough for me to squeeze through, if I manage to pry it open. Which, in my current state, is unlikely, because I wouldn't even be able to climb onto the towel rack with my injured ankle. But still, it's good to know for when I'm healed. This might be a way out.

My heart beats a little faster at that thought. A tiny spark of hope. Not enough yet to make me feel better about my situation, but at least it's a start.

I'm hungry, but I'm too exhausted to limp to the kitchen. I return to the bedroom and lie down with a relieved groan. I still haven't met a living soul in this house. The mutants don't count, and besides, they're not in charge and likely don't have any answers for me. I don't want that woman to return and sadly, I'm afraid of K7 coming to visit me too. Who I'd really like to chat to is that servant who was clearly unhappy with his life here. Maybe he's already started his new job, but his colleague didn't sound much happier. Even if they don't want to help me escape, I bet they'd be willing to give me some food.

For now, all I can do is wait. The pain is too much for me to sleep. I stare around the room, counting the cobwebs in the corner. I wish they'd left a book for me to read. Or some knives to sharpen. Anything to take my mind off things. Strangely enough, I still feel as imprisoned as I did back in my cell. My new nicer surroundings haven't changed that at all. Maybe this is even worse because I don't know what's going to happen. Is this the last moment of respite before they kill me?

I glare at the ceiling as if I could blame it for my predicament. But no, the only person I can blame for this - besides my captors - is myself. I walked right into the cage.

I kind of kidnapped myself. I invented the art of self-kidnapping. Now I just have to find out how to undo it. Self-rescuing. As much as I would love my guys to burst into the room right now to rescue me, it would hurt my pride a little. I think my pride would survive being assisted by cats though. None of those here yet. Maybe they didn't hear my call. Still, I have to hope.

I sit up and do my cat call again. And again. After five times, my throat hurts. I'm not used to using my voice for these kinds of frequencies.

A strange noise from the wall to my right makes me freeze. It's a quiet, faint noise, definitely not made by a human or even a cat. Something smaller.

I stop breathing and sit without even blinking.

It's a burrowing sound; claws against brick. Something is trying to get into the room. As quietly as I can, I breathe in through my nostrils, analysing even the faintest trace of scents. A rodent. Not sure if it's a mouse or a rat. I cringe. Usually, this would be dinner, but not today. The animal clearly heard my call. It was quiet until I called for feline help, and I don't believe in coincidences.

I hold my breath again and wait. The burrowing becomes more frantic until a piece of stone falls onto the wooden floor. It crashes into the silence, and even though my rational mind tells me nobody outside this room would have been able to hear it, my heart still beats a little faster.

I hear claws on wood before I see her. A mouse, a juvenile still, at the cusp of adulthood. Her grey fur is ruffled and covered in dust. Her nose twitches a couple of times, then she sneezes. How adorable. She wipes her face with her front paws, then looks around. At first, she ignores me, but when she realises that I'm the only living being in the room, she slowly approaches me.

She squeaks when she's a few foot away from me, as if to make sure I was the one that called her.

I stay as still as possible while repeating my cat call, just quieter than before. I had no idea other animals could understand it. Not that I've ever tried talking to a mouse before. I didn't really need to hear their cries of mercy before I ate them. And now this mouse may be my way out of here. How ironic.

When I talk to cats, they send me images and emotions rather than words. Maybe I can do the same with the mouse.

I concentrate and send her an image of the sky combined with the feeling of sunlight warming my fur. Almost immediately, the mouse sits up on her hind legs and sniffs the air, almost as if she's expecting to smell the outside world.

"Yes, outside. Do you know the way?"

She drops down to all fours and runs back to the hole where she came from.

"No, wait!"

I picture myself stuck in the tiny hole and pass that image on to the mouse. Her nose twitches in amusement.

"I need another way out. And I don't want any of the humans to see me."

She crooks her head as if in thought. Am I interpreting too much into her behaviour? Maybe she's just a stupid animal who's only steered by instincts, not conscious thought. It almost hurts to think that, since it would mean that my hope of the mouse showing me the way out is in vain.

"Can you do it?" I whisper. I hug myself as hopelessness creeps up on me again. I can't give up. Not yet.

An image pops into my head, but it's not created by

me. Giant blades of grass, taller than me, swaying in the wind. Moss-covered earth beneath my paws. The scent of daisies all around me.

I want to cry with relief. The mouse understands me and she knows a way outside.

WHISKERS
by Alicia Shipler

CHAPTER FIVE

If anyone would have told me I'd one day make friends with a mouse, I would have stabbed them.

Not anymore.

Whiskers - that's what I've started to call her - has a wicked sense of humour. For a mouse, anyway.

For the past few hours, she's shown me images of the inhabitants of the house. K7, the man who semi-kidnapped me, the woman who thinks she's K7's mother, about ten different mutant grunts and four servants. Whiskers is only sending me pictures and smells, not voices, so I don't know which of the servants are the ones who I overheard talking when I first woke up in this room. Not that I'm complaining. She's been such a big help. Step by step, I'm building a mental map of the house. It's a little hard because I'm seeing everything from the perspective of a tiny mouse, but it's enough to show me the potential escape routes. My main problem is that I'm not alone here. Those grunts could be waiting for me again. And the second problem is that I'm sure I'm being watched. I bet they're sitting somewhere upstairs with a large bowl of popcorn, pissing themselves laughing at my feeble attempts to escape.

Thanks to Whiskers, I now know that I'm downstairs in a tall building. It's hard to count the floors from the perspective of a mouse, but I bet it's at least ten storeys. There's one basement below me, but the mouse has only been in there once. I bet that's where they kept me until I was transferred to this room. The ground level is three floors above me. It's a long way to get to the exit, even if I was in top condition.

Whiskers moves through tunnels in the brickwork, but of course I wouldn't fit in there. She's shown me images of some ventilation shafts, but they don't start getting big enough for me until one level above me. That means I have to use the normal stairs, unless I find a convenient hole in the ceiling somewhere. I wish. Still, I'm further than I was when I woke up today. And I'm feeling a lot more confident. I'll make it out of here. I will.

Footsteps in the distance alert me, but Whiskers is faster. She disappears beneath the bed. I'm glad she doesn't leave the room. I don't want to be alone, even if my only company is a mouse.

I sit up as straight as I can and stare at the closed door in both anticipation and dread. If it's some of the grunts, they'd be able to simply pick me up and do whatever they want with me. As creepy as the woman was, I kind of hope it's her.

But no. The door opens and a very familiar face peeks in. K7. Usually, I prefer to think of my fellow clones as sisters, but not with her. Not after what I saw in my dream.

She walks into the room and closes the door behind her. A smile curves her pale lips, but it seems more like a habit than happiness. Her right eye, the mechanical one, glints and a red light shines from it, pointing right at me. What the fuck?

"What's that?" I challenge her. I doubt we need introductions.

"Hold still," she orders coldly. Her voice is nothing like my own. There's no life to it. She sounds much older than I am. In a twisted way, it reminds me a little of Grandma Doctor, the woman who created us.

"What are you doing?"

"Scanning you. Don't move or it might hurt."

I glare at her but I follow her advice. I'm in no mood for more pain.

"Your ankle is broken," she said dispassionately. "You need to take better care of yourself."

I can't help it, I snort out a laugh. "I'd be in much better condition away from here. Want to let me go?"

For a second, a child's fearful expression passes over her face, but then she's back to robot mode.

"You will stay. My parents have plans for you."

I shudder when she calls them her parents. "Do you know who I am to you?" I ask, keeping my voice as neutral as possible.

"Of course. You're the runaway."

"That's not what I meant. But yes, I like running away. Would love to do it now, actually."

"You're the experiment," she says with distaste. "You failed and disappointed my parents, so then they had me instead. I'm not a disappointment like you."

Ouch, that hurts even though I couldn't care less what her pretend-parents think of me. It's the way she looks at me, all high and mighty. She really thinks she's better than me. And not just that. The disdain in her eyes is clear. They've brainwashed her.

"I'm your sister," I say softly. "We're sisters."

"No, we're not. I don't have siblings. My parents say that I'm so perfect that they didn't need any other children."

Arrogant, much? This is ridiculous. I try to feel pity for her, but it's getting harder and harder.

"Have you always lived here with them?"

"No, we were in Attenburgh when I was younger, but then my father got a job here in Parseldon-"

She stops, her eyes widening. Oops. She's said too much.

Parseldon. The town closest to the capital city. This is where all the rich people and politicians live. Close enough to the capital to commute there for work, but far enough not to have to live alongside the plebs. I've seen pictures of Parseldon. Sleek buildings, large public parks, a river with water so clear you can drink it. I've never had any plans to go there. Not my kind of people, and too much security for assassins to go about their work unchallenged.

It's quite a distance from Attenburgh. A day of travelling if you're not running as a panther. My heart sinks at the thought. That makes it even less likely that my family can find me here. They might still be combing through Attenburgh, while I'm being kept in a town far away. Why can't life just be simple for once?

"What's your father's job?" I ask casually.

"I should be asking the questions," she replies haughtily. "I'm the one in charge."

I raise an eyebrow. "And what makes you think you're in charge?"

I shouldn't bait her, but I can't help it.

Her right eye glows red again. A ray of light touches my shoulder and I scream out in pain as it pierces my flesh. I clutch my shoulder, expecting there to be blood or at least a burn wound, but I feel nothing but smooth skin. What by all things evil is that thing?

"Did that hurt?" she asks innocently. "That was the lowest setting. Please don't make me use the higher one. That one hurts me too."

"Then why would you use that, if it causes you pain?"

A shadow crosses her face. "Sometimes, you have to feel the pain you're causing others."

It sounds like something she's heard so often that it's become a mantra for her. I doubt it's what she really thinks. Pity rises in me. It seems like she's had to use her strange eye as a weapon against her will.

"Have you always had that eye?" I ask her.

"Yes. It's pretty, isn't it? I can change its colour, look."

Suddenly, she's a child again. The eye flickers from red to green to bright yellow.

I smile to encourage her. I don't want her to turn psychopath again. Having her behave more like a child is much easier to deal with.

"What's your favourite colour?"

"Purple. What's yours?"

"Red. Purple is lovely too, though. Do you have a lot of purple things?"

She shakes her head. "No, my mother says I shouldn't favour one colour over another. It's just like with the servants. I'm not supposed to like one more than the others. She says I should feel the same for everything."

"That sounds very hard."

K7 nods. "It is. You won't tell her about purple, right? If she knew, she'd take the colour from my palette like she did with light blue."

Anguish tinges her voice. What a strange life this girl has. She seems well looked after physically - ignoring the mechanical eye - but they seem to have fucked with her mind somehow.

"I won't tell her," I promise. I mean it. She may be crazy and slightly twisted, but she's also my sister. "What's your name?"

She looks down at the floor. "That's a secret."

"Hey, I can keep a secret. I won't tell your mother about your favourite colour and I won't tell her that you told me your name. Deal?"

"I shouldn't."

"Come on, I'll tell you mine, too."

"I already know yours. You're Kat."

I grin. "But do you know my full name?"

She looks up at me. "Katriona."

"That's still not my full name."

She bites her bottom lip. Now she looks her age. She's clearly debating hard whether to confide in me or not.

I let her think in silence. I don't want to pressure her too much. I'm slowly getting her on my side and I don't want to put that in jeopardy.

"My mother calls me baby, but that's not my real name," she whispers. "And my father calls me K.C."

I'm not sure if she means Kacey or K.C. I really hope it's the former and not an abbreviation of something like Kat Clone.

"But Lynda calls me Puppet."

"Who's Lynda?" I ask.

"One of the servants. She's not my favourite, I promise."

I hold up my hands. "I never assumed that, don't worry. Which name do you prefer? Baby, Kacey or Puppet?"

She looks down on the floor again, evading my eyes. "Neither. I've made my own."

My sister seems scared of my reaction to that. Poor thing.

"Hey, look at me." She does it so fast that I know it's just an instinct. She's used to following orders. "I made my own name too. When I grew up, I was always just called Kat or Katriona, but then I learned that most humans have two names. A first name and a last name. So I came up with my own surname. Feln. Can you guess what's that based on?"

"Feln," she repeats. "Feline?"

"You got it right away, well done. Not many people figure it out at first try."

She smiles at me proudly. I somehow doubt that she gets praised a lot.

"Sophie," she blurts. "It's from a book I read. Not my favourite book, I promise."

I cringe but keep my expression neutral. "Sophie is a lovely name. I'll call you Sophie from now on if you want."

She nods. "But only when we're alone."

"Of course. I promise. Do your parents know you're here talking to me?"

She shakes her head and gives me a sheepish smile. "They kept saying that I could visit you soon, but it never happened. They think I'm doing my homework. My father is away for work and my mother's out shopping. It's only the guards and the servants here and they'd never tell on me."

I file that away for the future. It doesn't quite correspond with what I heard the servant woman say about the Little Mistress biting her arm, but who knows. Maybe Sophie doesn't always control her actions. Maybe she's a bit like Caitlin used to be before we came up with the right medication for her. I'll have to wait and see before

I jump to conclusions. For now, it's already a great success that the two of us are talking.

"Do they leave you alone a lot?" I ask.

Sophie shrugs. "Sometimes. But even if they're away, they can always eye me."

"What?"

She points at her mechanical eye. "They can eye me. It's like a telephone inside my eye. They can talk to me and see what I see. And make me do things. Sometimes everything goes black when he does that and I wake up later. I can't remember what happened or what I did."

I can't suppress a shudder. I thought she was lucky because she didn't wear a collar. Turns out, they've basically put the collar in her eye. I have no idea how it works, but I bet it will be a lot harder to remove than K7's collar. I can't just rip out this girl's eye.

"Could they be watching us now?" I ask carefully.

To my relief, she shakes her head. "No, I always know just before they do. I'll have about three seconds to run out of the room. It used to be without warning, but I've become better at dealing with it."

She squares her shoulders, clearly proud of her bravery.

"Well done," I praise her, and her chest gets even more puffed up. "That's very clever of you."

"I don't like it when they eye me," she admits. "But my father says it's the price of letting me see again. Everything has a price, even if it hurts to pay it."

Again, a sentence I bet she didn't come up with herself. Talking of them potentially watching us through her mechanical eye makes me realise the urgency though.

"Sophie, I need to ask you something. Do you know why I'm here?"

She cocks her head to one side, visibly confused. "Of course. You're going to be my friend."

"I'm sure that can't be the only reason?"

"It is! I told my mother that I wanted a friend and then my father took me to collect you the next day. They were really happy to bring you here, just like I was. We're going to be a family."

I try not to show her what I think of that plan. I've already got a family. I want to make her part of that family, but I'm certainly not going to join hers. I doubt her parents' reasons are as simple as she thinks. There must be more to it.

My stomach growls, interrupting my thoughts.

"You're hungry," she says knowingly. "That's good. My mother says it's important for you to be hungry. And you're supposed to scream a lot too, it helps to get rid of all the bad memories you have."

I blink at her. "Bad memories?"

"Yes. I have them too. It's hard to push them away sometimes. But she says that screaming helps. I watched you scream. You did very well."

I'm trying very hard not to react to her words. I kind of want to puke. They've totally brainwashed her. At the same time, I'm glad she didn't actually enjoy watching me suffer. She thought it was helping me. It doesn't make sense to me, but she seems to believe it. I don't want to disrupt our burgeoning relationship so I don't point it out to her that I was in agony when she watched me.

"I think your mother is wrong about being hungry," I say instead. "I'll be too weak to talk with you soon if I don't eat anything."

"But she's never wrong," Sophie protests. "My mother is always right."

Groan. "Maybe she forgot that I'm a shifter? Maybe

being hungry is good for humans, but not for shifters like us. Do you like being hungry?"

She shakes her head and a look of doubt flits across her face.

"See, I don't like being hungry either. How about you get us some food and we'll have it here together? Like a picnic?"

Her eyes widen. "A real picnic? I've never had one, but I've read about those. Can we have a blanket too?"

I can't help but smile at her sudden enthusiasm. "We can put this duvet on the floor, that's even comfier than a normal blanket. You go and get the food while I prepare everything here."

She nods and runs out of the room. My smile wavers a little. I shouldn't have picnics with her. I should somehow persuade her to get both of us out of the house and make a run for it. Instead, I slowly slide out of bed and drag the duvet down onto the floor while trying hard not to put any weight on my injured ankle. Maybe it'll heal faster after I've eaten.

I sit down on the blanket and listen for any signs that Sophie got caught.

Whiskers the mouse squeaks from under the bed.

"Yes, I know. This is all one big mess."

CHAPTER SIX

Sophie returns with a large basket full of food. My mouth waters the instant she enters the room. It's hard to hold back from pouncing at her and ripping the basket out of her hands. Patience, kitty.

She spreads out the food on the blanket. I've never seen anything tastier. I snatch a sausage roll and stuff it into my mouth, barely chewing before swallowing. Another suffers the same fate.

"I like them too," Sophie remarks, completely unaware that I'm eating them with such enthusiasm because I'm starving. Usually, I'm not even a big fan of sausage rolls. I prefer my meat juicy and without dough to distract from its flavour. "Try the dumplings."

She doesn't have to tell me twice. Three dumplings disappear into my mouth in record time, followed by meatballs, a massive piece of cheese and a couple of cocktail tomatoes. Only once I've added a piece of apple cake to the mix do I feel sated enough to take a break from stuffing my face. My stomach feels a little too full; I'm no longer used to eating as much as I want. Once I'm out of here, I'm going to buy myself a whole suitcase full of junk food and will spend a day demolishing it.

"You should try the rhubarb pie," Sophie encourages me. "The cook made it this morning."

"In a moment. Is that your favourite?"

Her face falls. "No," she says quickly. "I don't have a favourite."

My heart clenches at the sight of her trying to follow her mother's ridiculous rules.

"It's alright," I soothe her. "You can tell me what you really think. You don't have to pretend with me. And I promise that I will do the same. We don't have to lie to each other."

"I never lie," she protests, but it's easy to see she's not telling the truth.

"Do you want a secret?" I ask to prove to her that I mean it.

She nods eagerly.

"I miss being outside."

Again, she nods. "Me too. They've not let me out of the house since we collected you. It's so boring here."

My seeds won't need much fertiliser; she might be easier to persuade than I anticipated.

"Have you thought about just going outside without your parents' permission?"

"Of course not," she protests, but her expression tells another story. Good. She's not quite as brainwashed as I'd feared. She still has some spirit left in her.

"Picnics should be done outside. This is great, but it would be much more fun in the sun. Should we do that next time? Take it all outside and sit on the grass?"

"There's no grass," she says gloomily. "I've always wanted a garden but there's no space. Too many houses around ours."

"I'm sure there's a park somewhere. And even if we have to sit on the pavement, that's more fun than in here. Right?"

Reluctantly, she nods. "Yes. It sounds like fun. We could get ice cream too. I love how ice cream melts in the sun."

I smile. "Me too. It's like lapping up milk, except that you can do it as a human without being looked at strangely."

"Yes!" she exclaims. "But when I behave too much like a cat, I have to go into the small room instead of my own room. I don't have any toys there. She makes me watch those boring films about humans until I swear that I don't want to shift."

That must be the room I saw in my dream. I'm glad it's not her permanent room. It didn't look comfy and not made for a child at all.

"Do they let you shift?" I ask curiously, although I'm dreading the reply already.

"Yes, but only in the lab. They don't want me to do it without anyone watching."

"The lab?"

"It's downstairs. I have to go there for tests a lot. I've got lots of illnesses and they need to make sure that I'm not getting worse."

I grit my teeth. I bet she's not sick in the slightest. I sniff the air. No, she doesn't smell like she's ill. But I don't want to destroy every one of her illusions just now. That can wait for later when we're safe and far away from here.

"Is the lab where you got that eye?" I ask, pointing to her mechanical eye.

"No, that was before we moved here. I can't really remember what happened. My mother says I got very sick and one of my eyes stopped working, so they had to put in a new one."

"And do you believe that?" I enquire gently.

She tenses but then shakes her head ever so slightly. "They could have given me a normal eye, right? Not one that makes me do things?"

"You're right. They could have, I'm sure. That's why you can't trust everything they say. I know parents expect you to think that they're right, but they're not." At her shocked expression, I quickly add, "Not always. About some things, they're definitely right. Like that you have to eat your vegetables."

Look at me, nutritionist extraordinaire. Surely catnip counts as a vegetable, right? That way, I definitely get my five a day.

She takes a bite from the rhubarb pie, seemingly mulling over everything I've said.

"I'd like to do this outside," she says after a few minutes' silence. "The two of us, together."

"Me too." It's not a lie. I'm starting to like her, now that I understand more about her upbringing and how they've manipulated her.

"When?" she asks.

I'm speechless. Did she just offer to break me out of here? Not in so many words, but I'm sure that even she can understand that I won't be coming back here, and I won't let her return either. She's young, but she's intelligent. Suffering brings wisdom. I bet some important, wise person once said that.

"Tomorrow?" I suggest. "That way, we don't have to wait very long. And since we didn't eat all of the pie, we can finish it then."

She looks longingly at the last quarter of rhubarb pie.

"Okay," she says with a sigh. "We'll save it for tomorrow."

My heart is beating a little faster. Freedom is close. And

now that I've had food, I'm feeling stronger already. If we have to confront some of the mutant guards, I may be able to fight. I wiggle my ankle. Ouch. Still not healed, but it's not as bad as before our improvised picnic.

"I've got lessons in the morning, but I can come in the afternoon. And you're not going to tell my parents, right?"

I look her straight in the eyes and shake my head. "No, I won't. Will you?"

She doesn't hesitate. "Of course not. That wouldn't make sense."

Sophie wrinkles her nose in a rather patronising way. I suppress a grin. She's going to fit in well into the Kat family. Once we're reunited with the others, I might take her to Aunt Rose, who's still looking after the twins and Little Kat. Unless things have changed while I was imprisoned here. Something could have happened to them. The Pack...

No. I push that thought away. I can't think about stuff like that. I need to focus.

Suddenly, Sophie jerks, her healthy eye going wide.

"He's about to watch," she hisses, panic spreading across her face.

"Run. I'll clean up, you just run and pretend you weren't here."

She nods, tense as a bowstring, and runs from the room as fast as she can. I hope she was right about the delay in her father seeing through her mechanical eye. If he saw her sitting with me...everything would be lost. They'd probably put me back in my prison cell, or continue whatever mindfuck games they were playing here.

Nothing I can do about it now. I clean up our picnic, taking a nibble on this and that while doing so. I pocket some of the dry foods for later and shove everything else under the bed to hide the evidence. I'm tired from all the eating. Once my duvet is back on the bed, I lie down and curl up in a comfortable position.

A crunching noise from below the bed lets me know that Whiskers has started her very own picnic.

"I may not need your help after all," I say quietly. "But stay close, just in case."

She sends me an image of her bathing in a bowl of soup, using a piece of bread as soap. Okay then. She's got one weird sense of humour. I like it. I never thought I'd become friends with a mouse, but I think Whiskers and I are on the way to something akin to friendship. The relationship is definitely past the possibility of me eating her. And that's almost friendship, right?

Now that I'm sated, tiredness is rolling over me like a pleasant wave. I should try to stay awake, but I need to recharge my batteries and there's no better way to do that than sleep.

"Watch out for me, little one. Wake me when someone approaches the room."

Whiskers peeps happily and continues munching away.

For the first time since I woke up in this room, I fall asleep naturally, without being knocked unconscious. It feels rather good.

CHAPTER SEVEN

I sleep, eat, and sleep some more. It's a pleasant change from being starved and tortured. Whiskers stays with me, either beneath the bed or on the pillow beside me, only napping when I'm awake. She's a great companion. Are all mice this intelligent? If so, I almost feel bad for all the rodents I've eaten in the past.

My inner clock is telling me that it's almost twenty-four hours since Sophie and I had our picnic. I'm starting to get a little worried. Did her parents find out about our meeting? Are they punishing her just now? Or did she change her mind?

There's nothing I can do. My ankle has fully healed overnight, so I could walk around the house, but I don't want to risk it. If some mutant guards manage to knock me out now, all my plans are for nothing. No, I need to be patient and just hope that Sophie will come soon.

To distract myself, I do some stretches, forcing my body into submission. Everything aches, but I need to get my muscles back into shape. I've lost a lot of weight and muscle mass. I doubt I was this skinny even as a child, and that says a lot. They never gave us enough food at the Pack, but at least we had the chance to go scavenging once we'd done the kills of the day. Lennox and I would meet under the bridge, our favourite hiding spot, and would share whatever food we'd managed to find. My heart hurts at the memory. I miss him so much. I miss all of them.

You never know what you have until it's taken from you. I never understood how lucky I was to have those three guys. Men who really cared for me. And I for them. Did I ever tell them how much they meant to me? I'm not sure. Once we're reunited, I'm going to tell them. I might even use the L-word. Maybe.

A sound in the distance automatically makes me go into my favourite pouncing pose. I smirk. My body hasn't forgotten everything yet. And now that I've eaten, I might be able to fight. Not the way I used to, but I should be able to defend myself. I can't get involved in a fight though. I need to conserve my energy for running away. I doubt they're just going to let me go. They'll pursue me, us, and I need stamina for that.

Footsteps are coming closer. Two people. A child and an adult. Fuck. Sophie must have been caught.

I grab the two metal forks that Sophie brought along with the picnic, and ready myself for a fight. I'm not going to let them hurt her.

Whiskers jumps down the bed and hides beneath it, but I know she's watching me. I wish I could tell her to bring a message to my family, but I know Ryker's cats would eat her before she ever got the chance.

"Stay safe," I whisper. "Look for a better home than this."

I tiptoe to the door and wait for them to enter. If I'm fast enough, I might be able to knock out the adult, but that will only work if Sophie isn't under their control. If she starts fighting me, I'm screwed. I can't hurt her.

It's hard to scent them through the closed door so it's only when they've almost reached my room that I can get a proper reading on the adult. It's not one of Sophie's parents. I relax a little. It's not one of the grunts either; they barely have any scent, but this woman sweats so much that I want to pick my nose to get rid of the smell. The woman is nervous, very much so.

I lower my forks a little. If I'm lucky, this human is an ally rather than a foe. Sophie doesn't smell like she's under duress. For once, I might be in luck. Still, I stay next to the door so that I'll be hidden behind it when they enter the room. It's always the safest spot when trying to stay unseen long enough to assess a situation.

To my surprise, they knock on the door. How polite.

"Come in," I call out with a muffled voice so that it sounds as if I'm further inside the room.

I stop breathing when they open the door, ready to pounce if necessary. The woman enters behind Sophie, a little hesitant.

"Where is she?" the woman asks and I recognise her voice. She's the servant I heard on the first day I woke up here. The one who complained that she hadn't been allowed to wash me. Last time I regained consciousness, I'd been bathed and dressed in new clothes, so they must have changed that rule. I wonder if it was her who did that. However, I also remember her of complaining that Sophie had bitten her. That makes her a lot less trustworthy.

The girl sucks in a breath and walks around the door, following her nose. She smiles at me.

"Are we playing hide and seek?"

"Who's she?" I ask instead.

"That's Cook. She's made a picnic for us."

I frown at Sophie. "Didn't we agree not to tell anyone?"

The woman clears her throat and I realise I've not paid her any attention. I guess that's rude, but to be honest, I couldn't care less just now. In matters of life and death, politeness is a useless notion that only wastes time.

"I think I know what you're planning," the woman says, her voice shaking a little. She's afraid of me. "And I want to help. I've got a new job and today's my last day here. I have nothing to lose."

Her heartbeat tells a different story. She knows that if we're caught, she'll get punished. Or worse. I wouldn't be surprised if Sophie's parents would kill the woman for helping us. But I won't reject her help.

"Thank you," I force myself to say. "How can you aid us?"

A tiny smile curves her lips. "A distraction. I'll set fire to the kitchen. Let's burn this place down."

I look into her eyes to see if she means what she's saying. And yes, she does.

I give her a small nod. "Sounds good. How many people are in the building? Are Sophie's parents here?"

"No, they're away on business. They were supposed to return yesterday but they messaged to say that they'd be delayed. I think they're in Attenburgh to meet Peter Tamari."

"Wait, I know that name. What does he look like?"

The woman frowns. "Quite ordinary. Not exactly a looker. Late fifties. Grey hair. A scar beneath one of his eyes."

That's the siren Lily mentioned, the one who she accompanied to the Jewellers' Guild ball. It feels so long ago now. Stealing the diamond, working for the mayor, Lady Lara, finding that cute little fawn... Back then, we'd been wondering if Tamari was the siren who'd orchestrated the assassination attempt on me. I shudder at the memory. That poison was awful.

"If they're gone, who is here?" I ask to distract myself.

"It's just us, two other employees plus the usual guards."

I assume that with 'guards' she means the mutant grunts. "How many?"

"When you were still...below, we only had six of them around at all times. Now it's twelve."

She looks at me as if that's my fault. I didn't miss her slight pause though when she talked about *below*. The cell they kept me in must be on a lower level.

"Are there any other prisoners?" I ask out of interest. Not that I have the time or energy to save anyone else.

"No. You were the first in a long time. Lord Delaney changed his methods a couple of years ago."

Lord Delaney. This is the first time I hear his name. I don't like it. It sounds too pretty for the man who kidnapped and tortured me. Who turned Sophie into this. I wonder why he's called Lord. We've not had a monarchy in centuries. In Attenburgh, Lady Lara had that title because she was the mayor. Is Delaney a mayor here too? Or some other powerful official? It wouldn't surprise me.

"Shall we have our picnic?" Sophie is jumpy with impatience.

I smile at her. "Yes, let's do it. Do you know what the weather's like?"

"It's cloudy but there's no rain."

That means there are windows further up in the house. Or maybe she just watched the weather report, but let's hope it's the former. I can't bear the thought of my little sister growing up in a house without windows.

The cook leads us out of my room and through the corridors I'm already familiar with. I hope she knows where the guards are so that we can avoid them. Maybe she's even told them to stay away. I don't want to get my hopes up, but if this ends well, I might give her a job at M.E.O.W. We could always do with a cook.

I get a little wary when we walk up the stairs that I was pushed down during my last exploration, but nobody stops us. Everything is quiet, no matter how much I strain my ears. Sophie doesn't show any fear, but the cook makes up for that. Sweat pools on her back, gluing her blouse to her skin. Her heart is beating fast but, to her credit, her expression doesn't give away her anxiety. I guess she's used to hiding her feelings in this household.

We sneak through the house, ascending floor by floor until a blast of fresh air reaches me. Wow. After months inside windowless rooms, I'd forgotten what air smelled like. We must be close to the exit now.

I itch with the temptation to just run and run without ever looking back. Freedom is so close. If only I could do that, but I went through this whole ordeal to save my sister and there's no way I'm abandoning her now.

When we pass a kitchen - much larger than the one I saw downstairs - the woman stops and collects a big picnic basket. She lifts the lid just enough for me to get a quick look at the contents. Knives, wrapped food, two bottles. I'm having trouble to believe that she's helping us. That we might get out of here alive and in one piece. How did someone *nice* get to work here?

"Thank you," I mutter and I mean it. Every single letter.

"Is there rhubarb pie?" Sophie asks, unaware of what's going on. It's interesting how she can be this innocent one moment and behave much older than her age the next.

"Of course," the woman says not unkindly. When I overheard her, she complained about Sophie having bitten her, but she must realise that my little sister can't help behaving like she does. Not after all her supposed parents have done to her.

The cook checks her watch. "Time to go, their break is almost over. There are some shoes by the door, hopefully they'll fit. Get as far away from the house as you can, I'm going to try and make this one big firework."

Something akin to excitement crosses over her lined face.

I bow my head. "Thank you. Be safe."

"You too. Look after Sophie."

The girl in question looks up at us both. "Are we not coming back?"

There is both hope and fear in her eyes.

I take her hand and squeeze it. "No. We're not. We have a new life waiting for us."

CHAPTER EIGHT

I can barely breathe when I step out of the building.
Free, at last.

We're surrounded by houses, most of them a lot smaller than the tower-like structure I've been held in. Too many possible eyes on us. We need to get out of here as fast as possible.

"Let's have our picnic in a quiet spot. Do you know one? Maybe a forest?"

"The Duchess Woods," Sophie suggests, her normal eye sparkling with excitement. "It's not far."

"Good. Shall we have a race there? I'll take the picnic basket to make it fair."

She scoffs. "I may be smaller, but I bet I'm faster than you even if I'm carrying the basket. But alright then. First to get to the Woods gets the rhubarb pie."

And she starts running.

With a grin, I follow her. I keep my senses on high alert, very aware of how exposed we are. People could be watching us from their homes. People who're friends of Lord Delaney, or even other sirens. It's not safe, but there's nothing I can do about it but get out of this settlement as soon as possible.

Stretching my legs feels amazing. A fresh breeze strokes my hair while sunshine warms my face. Most of the houses have small gardens filled with sweet-smelling flowers and their scent almost makes me want to cry. I've missed this so much. Nature. Freedom.

Even in my weakened state, I have no trouble matching Sophie's speed, but I let her lead, staying close behind her. Hopefully, if the neighbours do see us, they'll think us two girls having fun on a sunny day. That's certainly true for Sophie. Her happiness surrounds her like a second set of clothes, bright and beautiful. In turn, I'm happy for her. She deserves this moment of happiness. Who knows when we next get a chance to laugh.

After a few minutes of running, we reach the edge of the village. The houses here are smaller and nowhere near as well looked after as the ones earlier. We pass a ruined building to our right before the forest welcomes us home.

It feels like that. Home. The cat in me is itching to get out. Not yet. We need to get to safety first. Far away from Lord Delaney's house. If I shift now, I'm not sure if I'll stay in control. The panther might take over and I'd be no use to Sophie that way. I might even be too weak to shift in the first place.

Sophie stops at an old birch, panting slightly.

"I win!"

I grin. "Yes, you do. The pie is all yours. But let's run some more, okay? We don't want to be interrupted."

She shoots a wistful look at the picnic basket but then nods. "Where are we going?"

"How big is this forest?"

"Big. We might have to run for two hours to reach the other end."

I raise an eyebrow at her. "Are you afraid of a challenge?"

Again, she looks at the basket. She really wants that pie.

"No. I'll beat you," she says, pushing back her shoulders and puffing up her chest. "I'm the fastest girl in Parseldon."

"Then let's prove that. First to the other side gets the sausage rolls."

* * *

"I DIDN'T WANT THEM ANYWAY."

This time, I didn't let her beat me. It took most of the energy I'd gained over the last twenty-four hours though. I'm exhausted. I need a break, and besides, I don't think I could stop Sophie from finally having her picnic. I think she knows that we're running away. She's too clever not to realise, but pretending that it's all just a little excursion will make it easier for her to deal with. I keep having to remind myself that she won't be able to shake off her captors' influence just like that. It will take time.

We sit down and start gorging ourselves on the food the cook prepared for us. Sophie doesn't comment on the knives in the basket. She's only interested in the rhubarb pie. At least I know how to bribe her in future. This girl will do anything for a slice of pie. Hopefully, Caitlin can bake some. If not, she'll have to learn. There's no way I'm standing in the kitchen, baking. I'd probably burn the place down.

By the time my stomach has reached a satisfying level of fullness, I'm having to fight a wave of tiredness. No time to sleep. We need to get more distance between us and Parseldon. By now, they'll have likely noticed our absence.

They will be coming after us. The forest is too dense to use horses, but those grunts will be at least as fast as us, and I doubt they'll stop for a picnic.

"Sophie? What happens if you cover your eye?"

"I'm not allowed to." She grimaces. "Father doesn't like it."

"But you've done it before, haven't you."

"Yes. Once. But I promised him never to do it again."

The anguish on her face tells of the punishment she must have faced. Poor thing. But I have to know more.

"Can he still make you do things even if he can't see through your eye?"

She nods. "But it's harder for him. Right now he can't reach me anyway."

Confusion battles relief. "How? I thought distance wasn't an issue? He was able to eye you yesterday even though he wasn't home."

"The antenna isn't here, silly," she tells me as if that should be obvious. He needs the antenna to send the signal. He once explained to me how it all worked. He either needs to be close to me or I need to be close to the antenna."

"So that means he definitely won't be able to control your eye?"

She shakes her head, clearly very happy about that fact. "No eyeing. It's just us." Her smile disappears. "We're not going back, are we?"

"No, we won't. I'm going to take you to my home. You'll be safe there. You'll get to meet my friends and our sisters. And lots of cats."

"Sisters?"

Ah. She doesn't know. "I'll explain later. We should leave."

"Where is your home?"

I can't help but sigh. "Attenburgh. At least we'd just made our home there before I was taken. I don't know if they're even still there. We need to find a phone so I can find out. If they're still in Attenburgh, we'll have to find a way to get there."

"When we went to see you, we took the train."

Bless her innocence. See me. Not quite what I would call kidnapping. She was used as the bait and didn't even realise it.

"I'd love to take the train, but only rich people get to take it."

"I'm rich."

She's not boasting, she's merely stating a fact. She'll have to drop that attitude though. While I have money, there's always something I need to spend it on. And I'm not talking expensive jewellery and jacuzzis. More like a malfunctioning morgue or new lab tools for Bethany.

"Do you have any money on you?" I ask. It's a rhetorical question, but to my surprise, she nods.

"I don't know if it's enough for the train though."

She pulls out a bunch of notes from her skirt pocket. I think my eyes are about to pop out of my head. That must be at least a thousand darems. Where did she get that kind of money?

When I ask her, she just shrugs. "My mother pays me pocket money, but I never get to go out so I can't spend it. Sometimes Cook bought me something, but never enough to really get rid of my money."

Her fake mother must have been compensating for the lack of maternal care. I'd usually have to do at least twenty hits for this kind of sum, and that's without expenses like poison top-ups and extortionate amounts of laundry detergent. Of course, the only one that effectively deals with blood stains is also the most expensive.

With her money, we might actually be able to afford the train, but I doubt that's a very stealthy way of travelling. Only the rich and famous use the train that criss-crosses the country like a compass rose. Passengers will know each other. The two of us would stand out like a torn-off thumb. No, we have to travel the slow way. But first, I need to figure out if my family is still in Attenburgh.

"Is there a village nearby?" I ask Sophie. "I need to find a house to sneak in and use their telephone."

"I'm not sure. I don't think there's anything but fields around the Duchess Woods, but I've only been here a few times for hikes. And that was always with my parents so we didn't explore away from the paths."

"Then I'll guess we'll just have to walk and see. Once we're away from the forest, I might be able to sense any nearby humans."

The food has refilled my energy levels pretty quickly. My senses are getting stronger, as is my body. If I continue to be able to eat as much as I want, it shouldn't be too long until I'm back to normal. Hopefully. It's not as if I have experience with being almost starved to death while also being tortured physically and mentally. I'm sure this will leave some scars that won't show until later. Not something I should worry about now. We've got more pressing issues.

With most of our food gone, carrying a picnic basket around doesn't make much sense. I wish I had my normal clothes with all the pockets and not this flimsy dress they put me in. My calves are full of bloody scratches from the undergrowth and my feet hurt from the uncomfortable shoes the cook gave me. I shouldn't complain. I could still be naked and barefoot. Think positive.

We make our way to the edge of the forest. This time we're walking rather than running, both of us both full of food and exhausted. Darkness is closing in quickly.

"Where are we going to sleep?" Sophie asks the question I was posing myself.

"We're going to find somewhere safe. Not yet, though. We don't want the guards to find us, right?"

"No, they're not very nice. Some of them can't even speak. They only growl and attack without warning."

I should ask if they ever hurt her, but I don't want to know the answer. I'm pretty sure I already know. She's been damaged by everyone who's ever been around her, save maybe that cook and other servants. It's a miracle that she trusts me.

"Once we're home, we'll be safe from them," I promise. "We just need to get to a phone and find out where my friends are. Everything will be alright."

I wish I could believe my own words.

CHAPTER NINE

As soon as we leave the forest, my senses go into overdrive. Enemies could be lurking in every shadow. In the forest, the trees gave us some cover, but here we're exposed.

Fields spread out all around us, reaching far into the distance. Most are host to dried stalks of whatever the farmers harvested, some are completely empty. The harvest season must have been at least a month ago. Yet another reminder of how much time passed while I was imprisoned. I used to love harvest time. The market stalls would be full of ripe fruit, but Lennox and I often went straight to the warehouses, munching on whatever had fallen off the carts on the way there. Sometimes, we were sated by the time we got to the warehouse so we'd just sit down in a quiet corner and snooze.

I lead us through the fields with the most crop corpses. I know they don't offer enough cover, but it makes me feel a little less on edge nonetheless. The sharp stalks rip open the soles of my feet, but my shifter healing powers have grown back just enough to take the edge of the pain.

Sophie follows me without complaint, but she's wearing expensive-looking boots as well as trousers that protect her legs.

By the time the night envelops us in its cloak of darkness, we still haven't come across any signs of nearby humans. No houses anywhere to be seen. No fresh scents either. Luckily, Sophie's night vision seems to be as good as mine, so we trudge on. A full moon is shining above us. Lennox will likely be running right now. He's got his wolf under control, but during full moon nights, it's hard for him to stay human. In Attenburgh, we once ran together, all night until dawn, before shifting in a little meadow. We had great sex there. I can't help but smile. Sex after shifting is always the best. It's when my senses are still more intense and every touch creates explosions of pleasure in my mind.

"What are your friends like?" Sophie asks out of the blue.

"They're all very different, but they're also similar in what drives them. Some of us are usually solitary, but we somehow fit together like the pieces of a jigsaw puzzle. We've all got different backgrounds, but that doesn't matter. Gryphon is a siren and had a very privileged upbringing. He even went to university to study medicine. On the other hand, Lennox grew up with me in the Pack. We didn't have a lot of food as children, but we had each other and that helped a lot."

I continue telling her all about my men, then the M.E.O.W. employees. I have to fight tears when I think of them all. She listens intently, sometimes asking questions, but mostly just taking it all in. With every word, my heart breaks a little more. I miss them so much. It's been too long since I saw them. Touched them. My skin tingles at the thought. I've not touched another being ever since I got self-kidnapped. Strange. I never thought I'd miss being touched, even if it's just a handshake or a quick hug. I'm not even a hugger, but...

"I can smell something," Sophie interrupts my train of thought. "I think it's a human."

I still and breathe in the night air. She's right. At the very edge of my sensory range, I can detect the faint traces of a human male. He's old and sweaty.

"Well spotted. Let's head his direction, he might have a house we can use."

We're silent as we weave our way through the fields. More and more tracks start to appear between them, but we stick to the centre of the fields where we have a bit more cover. My feet hurt like crazy by now. Mud must have seeped into the cuts, preventing them from healing.

Though when lights come into view in the distance, the pain fades into irrelevance. A house. By the looks of it, it's a solitary farmhouse in the middle of nowhere. Perfect.

The closer we get, the surer I am that there's only the one man inside. Old smells of other people still linger in the air, but those are at least a day old. We should be safe here for the night. Now we just need to get rid of him so that we can relax and recuperate.

A large stable with a roof that looks rather leaky is next to the house.

"Wait here," I whisper to Sophie. "I'll check out our mark."

"Mark?"

Oh. I fell into my old pattern. This isn't an assassination. I'm not a murderer. As good as it would feel now to take a life, I should restrict myself to incapacitating him while we're here. I don't have my trusted poison darts, so I'll have to stick to manual, old-fashioned methods.

"Just a figure of speech," I mutter. "Wait here until I call for you."

Luckily, she's trained to follow orders and doesn't question me. Once we're home, I'll have to teach her to think for herself and occasionally break the rules. It's part of being a cat. We look at the rules and decide whether it's worth following them, but only if it gives us an advantage.

I sneak over to the farmhouse and crouch beneath an open window. A deep snore reaches my ears. That makes it even easier. Instead of squeezing myself through the window, I try the door. It's open. Guess what they say about rural life is true. People really don't lock their doors. It's almost disappointing, but in my current state, I should be grateful.

The house is old and smells of cow. I didn't sense any animals though, besides a coop of chickens, so they must either be grazing far away from here or he sold them. Dust covers most surfaces and the floor is stained with mud. The guy isn't someone who cares for his surroundings.

I tiptoe towards the snoring. His bedroom door is slightly open, giving me a view of the house's owner. He's in his seventies, has a shaggy beard and even shaggier eyebrows, and he's sleeping naked. Without a blanket. Thanks, I didn't need to see that. I've seen my fair share of men's dicks, but this one is a particularly ugly, wrinkly exhibit. I'm glad I didn't take Sophie with me.

He's fast asleep, making it easy for me to sneak up on him. I snatch one of the pillows next to him and press it against his face, making sure his eyes are covered. He struggles, but he's weak and quickly succumbs to the suffocation. I listen to his heartbeat and take off the pillow as soon as it's getting dangerously slow. I don't want him to die. Well, maybe I do, but it's not right.

I find some scarves in his wardrobe and tie him up. A

stained handkerchief serves as his gag. Hopefully, his unconsciousness will give way to sleep and he won't even remember what happened. When we leave in the morning, I'll untie him and he'll never knew who spent the night in his house.

Satisfied that he won't be any trouble, I call out for Sophie before exploring the house. I can smell the food in the kitchen, which is a nice bonus, but the true treasure is the phone in the dingy living room. Jackpot.

Without waiting for Sophie, I dial the M.E.O.W. headquarters number.

It rings once, twice, three times, then it finally picks up. I don't think my heart could have made it any longer than that.

"Hello? We're closed."

Lily's voice. My tear ducts are malfunctioning terribly. Has she always sounded this melodic? I could hug and kiss the shit out of her. But that's when Sophie enters the room and I try to keep my cool. She mustn't see me fall apart. I'm going to have to wait with that until later, when I'm alone.

"It's me." I choke out the words, barely able to speak.

"Kat?" She sounds unsure, but I can't blame her with how hoarse my voice is.

"Yes. It's me."

Something shatters in the background. She must have pushed something over. I've not known Lily to be clumsy, but this is a special occasion.

"Is it really you? We weren't sure-"

"We're close to Parseldon. Are you all still in Attenburgh?"

"Parseldon? How the heck did you end up there? And who's we?"

"My sister and I. It's a long story but we need to get

away from here as quickly as possible. My geography is rubbish, can you plot us a route to Attenburgh? We've got money but no weapons."

"Yes...sure...I can't believe it's you! Are you alright?"

"Of course I am." I almost snap at her. I don't want her to know how completely not-alright I am.

"I can tell even through the phone that you're lying. But that's okay. For now. We're going to talk about this when you're back home. Let me check the map, I think Gryphon is closest to you. The guys split up a couple of months ago to follow different leads. If we're lucky, he'll still be in Darrwin. Let me make a couple of calls. Are you in a safe place?"

"Yeah, we broke into an old guy's home. We should be okay here for the next couple of hours, but I want to leave at dawn. They'll be looking for us."

Lily sighs. "I have so many questions but I know this isn't the time and place. Let me make a couple of calls and find out who's closest to you. Then I'll draft you a route to meet them. We'll get you back here, don't worry."

"I can't wait," I admit. "It's not been like I imagined a holiday."

She laughs. "Trust me, I have hunted better targets than you. Some days I thought he'd simply killed you and disposed of your body. Cut it up or dissolved it in acid."

"Nope, I'm alive. With a complete body. All arms and legs are still intact."

"Thank goodness. I've got your number on my screen, so I'll call you back as soon as I know more. Even though I want to keep you on here because I still can't believe we're talking to each other."

I quietly agree. It feels surreal. After all the months of isolation, talking to Lily is both bliss and overwhelming.

After I hang up, I just stand there for a moment, lost in

thought. Sophie looks at me curiously but doesn't say anything. She seems to understand that I'm not going to talk about it all just now.

Gryphon might be in Darrwin. If I'm not completely mistaken, that's maybe two days away, if we walk and don't find faster transport. If we run or steal some horses...we could meet him tomorrow. Oh my poor, sweet heart. It's about to break from beating too fast. Stop being emotional, Kat. It doesn't suit you.

"I'll look for food," Sophie says and runs off, giving me the chance to do what I've been wanting to for the past few minutes. I sink to the ground and let go of those stupid tears.

CHAPTER TEN

We use the time waiting for Lily to call back by raiding the pantry and finding some clothes for me to wear. The old guy is a head taller than me and a little larger around the hips, but with a couple of adjustments and a wide belt I manage to make myself a new outfit. It immediately raises my confidence in that we will truly pull this off. I felt vulnerable in that awful dress, but with fabric around my body, it all seems more positive.

Sophie has found a backpack which, surprise, smells like cow. We've stuffed it with canned food and two extra water bottles, and have tied a blanket on top. Who knows if we'll find a house to stay in again tomorrow night. I don't get cold easily, but maybe Sophie does, and even if not, a blanket will make the ground a little more comfortable.

While I'm busy crafting myself some sheathes for the knives the cook gave me as well as a wicked looking axe I discovered in the basement, the phone finally rings. I launch myself at it as if it's prey.

"Lily?"

"No, it's Gryphon."

My heart stops. Ouch. Pull yourself together, Kat. This isn't the time to fall apart.

"Kat? Are you there?"

He sounds hungry. I get that. I crave him so much that if he was here, I'd pounce and ravish him from top to bottom. In a way that Sophie really shouldn't witness. Heat rises in me; the need to be touched.

"Yes, I'm here." My voice is hoarse and almost brittle.

"Shit, it's so good to hear your voice. When Lily called I thought she was fucking with me. You're back. How?"

"Long story. I'll tell you everything when we meet." No. I won't. I won't burden them with what happened to me. I'll give them the tame, condensed story, minus the torture.

"Lily said you're in Parseldon?"

"Yes, a day's walk from there. We ran all day and now we're holed up at a farm. Where are you?"

"The outskirts of Darrwin. I was going to make my way to Parseldon and then to the capital next. Seems I finally found a reliable trace, but you were faster. I can rent some horses and either ride to your farm or meet you in the middle."

"I don't want to stay here longer than we need to. I'm convinced they're hunting us, so we shouldn't linger. We'll sleep for a couple of hours and then leave."

"Good, head West until you get to the River Burn. No matter where you are just now, you can't miss it, you'll have to cross it on the way to Parseldon. There's a bridge upriver, with an inn on the other side. I'll meet you there."

I'm struggling to get my head around this. We might meet Gryphon tomorrow. In person. Touchable. I'll be able to hug him. Speak to him. Lick him.

Maybe not the last one, especially not in front of Sophie.

My cat purrs deep within me. Gryphon might not be a feline himself, but she's marked him as hers, just like the other two. And that means a lot. I never thought my cat would ever accept a mate, let alone three. She's way too independent and solitary. Well, not anymore.

"I can't wait to see you again," he says softly. "It's been too long."

I swallow hard. My throat is too constricted to reply. All that torture must have messed with my brain. I'm way too emotional. The walls I built around my feelings are almost non-existent. I'm vulnerable and I don't like it.

"See you soon," I croak. "If we can't stay at the inn, we'll leave a message."

"Who's we?"

"My sister and I."

It feels good to say that. Sophie must think the same for she smiles at me, her healthy eye shimmering with joy. She's finally found her real family, not the sirens pretending to be her parents while in fact abusing and brainwashing her. Looking at her makes me realise though that she'll stand out once we are amongst humans. We need to get something to cover that mechanical eye, something that isn't an eyepatch, since that would draw just as much attention on a young girl.

"Your sister. I'm glad you got her out too. What's her name?"

"Sophie. She chose that name, just like she chose the colour purple as her favourite. And she likes rhubarb pie. And she looks just like me when I was her age."

The words blurt out, a rambling mess. I better hang up the phone before my brain erupts through my mouth and I say stuff I shouldn't.

"When will you get to the inn?" I ask.

"Late afternoon, hopefully earlier, depending on how

quickly I can procure some horses. Does Sophie need her own one?"

"No, she can ride with me. She's small enough."

"I can ride," Sophie protests. "My mother took me to the stables to teach me."

I smile at her. "Yes, but we'll be faster and safer if we're together. You'll get your chance to show me your riding skills in the future, I promise."

That pacifies her, thank goodness. I'm surprised she likes to ride, though. I hate it and so do the horses. They sense that I'm not human and will instinctively react to having a predator sit on their backs. Still, it's the fastest way to travel besides the train. We could get a cart, but that would be slower and makes escaping away from roads a lot harder. Horses it is. We'll leave the train ride for another time, when we're not being pursued by mutant grunts and their siren masters.

"Two horses then. That shouldn't take too long. Stay safe, Kat, understood? Don't take any risks. I don't want to lose you again, not now that you're so close."

"Don't worry, I don't intend on being caught. We'll stay away from any settlements until we get to that bridge. Save us a seat and some ale, if you get there first. No, make that an apple juice for Sophie. I think she's too young for anything stronger."

She shoots me an insulted look, but there's no way I'm giving her any alcohol. I may not be the most responsible cat, but I do know that children shouldn't have intoxicating food or drinks. Catnip excluded. I'll be sure to introduce her to that once we're back home.

"Stay safe," he repeats before ending the call. I stare at the phone for a moment. My mind is a mess of happiness and worries. With my recent luck, we'll be caught a mile away from that bridge. I might even get to see Gryphon from a distance before they lock me up again. I ball my hands into fists. No, I'm not going to let that happen.

"Gryphon sounds nice," Sophie says with a smile. "I can't wait to meet him."

"If everything goes well, you won't have to wait very long. We better get some sleep so that we can run most of the way tomorrow."

She nods and yawns. It's almost as adorable as a kitten's yawn.

While she curls up on the sofa, I check on the old guy. He's still unconscious but breathing fine, so I leave him to it and join my little sister. Time to sleep and dream of being in Gryphon's arms.

I'M IN A WHITE ROOM. NO, NOT A ROOM. IT'S A WHITE space without walls or a ceiling. Nothing but white as far as the eye can see. I'm immediately aware that this is a dream, but that doesn't make it any less surreal. I'm standing on white but I have no shadow. I can't even tell if the ground is solid or something else entirely.

A faint memory tells me that I've been here before, but the memory feels wrong, like it isn't my own. I lift my hand to my eyes to rub them and touch cold metal. It's not me. I'm Sophie.

Am I in her dream or am I simply dreaming to be her?

A figure appears in the distance. His clothes are simple jeans and a black shirt, but in this desert of white, he's as colourful as a parrot that's fallen into several pots of paint.

He moves with grace; a predator like myself. There are no scents in this world so I have to rely on my eyesight, waiting for him to come close enough to see his features.

When he finally does, I involuntary take a step back.

It's the siren. Lord Delaney. Sophie's pretend father. A shiver runs over my back but it's not my own. Sophie is scared. Now I'm sure that she's in this body with me together. I send her some reassuring vibes, hoping that she'll somehow feel them, before turning my attention towards the siren.

He approaches without a care in the world, completely oblivious to the fact that I'm about to pounce and attack.

I have nothing to say to this man. There's no point in talking to him. All I want to do is make him suffer. Hurt him. Destroy him. Claw out his innards and feed them to him. Bite off his cock, rip out his spine. I lick my lips. It's time to put an end to this.

I jump, flying through the air in a perfect arch, shifting in mid-air, but before I can even touch him, I'm repelled by an invisible barrier and flung back. I manage to land on all fours, not as gracefully as I'd wanted but at least I'm immediately ready to try again.

The siren grins wolfishly but doesn't say anything.

Both Sophie's and my own anger combine into fury. We're going to wipe that grin off his face.

Again, we attack, this time from the ground, running straight at him, but again, there's something that stops us from getting to him. This time, we're better prepared and avoid being pushed back.

We roar and swipe at the invisible barrier. It's hard as glass and our sharp claws don't leave a scratch. We hiss in frustration.

"You don't stand a chance against me," the siren says calmly, but his voice is full of menace. "You never did. I made you. I raised you. I tamed you. And as long as you're under my control, you'll never be able to attack me."

"I'm not under your control," we snarl.

"But you are."

He raises his hand and a bright red light flashes between his fingers. Pain races through our skull, originating in the metal eye. Even in our shifted form, the fake eye stayed. We clutch our head with our paws, howling in pain. Memories tell me that this has happened many times before. It's why Sophie is scared to shift. Every time she did, she was given pain like now. Or worse. Her fear permeates my mind and no matter how much I try to push it back, it's slowly overpowering me.

Through the pain, I realise there's only one way to stop it. I have to get rid of the mechanical eye. I mentally ask Sophie for permission. She hesitates. She's tried it before. She failed. It ended in even more agony. But this time, it's not just her. We're together. Sisters, bound by more than just blood.

She agrees. We fight the pain, slowly moving our paws towards the eye. Extend out claws.

The siren screams together with us as we rip out the eye. Pain like I've never experienced crashes through our skull, burning our mind from the inside. But the eye falls to the white ground, splattering it with blood. It's out.

Warm liquid runs down our face, wetting our fur. We whimper with pain, but it's a different kind of pain now. It's natural. It's our body crying out in agony. It's not created by the siren. And with that knowledge, it's easier to bear. It will pass. We will heal. And then we'll be free.

"That was a mistake," the man hisses. "You're worthless to me now. Before, I would have taken care to capture you alive. You've just earned yourself a bounty on your head. Your dead head."

I want to attack him. I instinctively know that I'd be able to now. The barrier will be gone. But blood is still pouring from my empty eye socket and with it, my strength.

The white space turns red around the edges. I blink in confusion, and when I open my healthy eye, the siren has gone. It's just us now. Bleeding redness all over the white.

Despite the pain, I have to smile.

We're free.

I wake up with a gasp and jump from the armchair I'd been sleeping in. The dream is still vivid in my mind and with it, the worry for Sophie. She's turned away from me, her body curled up in a ball. She looks like she's sleeping, but her heartbeat tells another story.

"Sophie, turn around," I order.

A whimper is her only reply. I race to her side and gently force her to roll over, exposing her face.

The mechanical eye has gone. A gaping hole is where it used to be, gruesome to behold.

Fuck. How the hell did a dream just become reality?

Unlike in the dream, she's not bleeding as much. Yes, blood is slowly running down her face, but it's already getting less. She's healing fast, like any young shifter. I doubt she'll regrow the eye, but at least the wound will close. If we can find her a glass eye, she'll pass for a normal child. The first time since they put that monstrosity into her.

"How are you feeling?" I ask gently.

"Strange. Like something's missing."

I almost laugh in a hysterical sort of way. Yes, there's definitely something missing. Every village idiot would be able to tell you that.

"How do I look?"

I smile at her, hoping that will make her feel less anxious. "Like a true warrior who's just won a big battle. It will heal, don't worry. Are you in a lot of pain?"

"It's fine."

It clearly isn't, but she's brave. Just like any cat, she's hiding her pain. It's a necessity in the wild where both friend and foe could take advantage of your weakness.

"I'll get some wet cloth and maybe there's some ice in the freezer. Keep your eye closed, we don't want any dirt to get into the wound."

I only find one clean cloth in the cupboard under the sink and I don't have time to search anywhere else. It'll have to do. I grab a bag of frozen peas, hoping the bag is clean enough. At least the man's freezer is in better condition than his mouldy fridge.

As if he could hear my thoughts, the old guy suddenly shouts from his bedroom. The gag prevents him from articulating actual words, but it's clear that he's not happy. I sigh and return to Sophie. As soon as I enter the living room, her pained expression turns blank. Good girl. She's even stronger than I thought.

I clean her bloody face and the eyelid as best as I can, but I'm not willing to touch the hole where her eye used to be. I don't trust the cloth to be free of germs that could lead to infection. Besides, it's already healing. The blood flow has almost stopped, but I still press the bag of frozen peas against it to prevent any further bleeding.

Sophie puts her hand on mine. She's shaking a little, but it's so faint that most people wouldn't have noticed.

"Check on the old man," she whispers. "I'm fine."

I'm not convinced, but the screaming is becoming annoying, so with a last probing look, I leave her to it.

The man stops screaming as soon as I enter the room. His eyes are wide and bloodshot. He tries to shuffle backwards, but I've tied him up too well for him to move.

"Hhhhhrmpppfffff."

I raise an eyebrow.

"Hhhhrrrrrmmm."

Nope, I don't understand. But I should put him out of his misery. It's not his fault he lives in a house that we needed to occupy for the night.

I take another step forward, enjoying the fear in his eyes. I shouldn't, but I do. It's been too long.

"If I remove the gag, do you promise not to scream?"

For a second, anger and a hint of resistance flashes across his face, then he nods.

"Good. But first, I need you to know that I intend you no harm. I'm not going to hurt you. And I'm sadly not going to kill you either. As much as I'd like to, it would go against the last remains of my morals. Besides, my little sister is in your living room. I wouldn't want her to realise what I am. Not yet, anyway."

I pause for a moment. Do I want her to know that I'm an assassin? Would I want her to follow in my footsteps? With Little Kat, it was different. I want her to be a child, to have an education and hopefully live an almost normal life. It was too late for the twins and even though they're currently staying with Aunt Laura, I bet they're not going to choose a legal job in the future.

Sophie, however, has that feral side to her that would make her an excellent assassin. With some training, naturally, but she's already on a good way. Is it right, though? I might have to discuss it with Lily. She's a predator too, in her way, and loves to play with the men who are her prey, but her moral compass is better than mine. Maybe Gryphon too, he's got a sister himself.

The man clears his throat. Ah, yes. Focus on the present. The future will arrive when it's time.

"We're going to leave very soon," I continue. "We only needed a safe place for the night. Once we're ready to go, I'm going to untie you and then we'll be on our way. No need to call the authorities, right?"

He nods immediately, still scared to bits. I'm amazed he hasn't peed himself yet. Don't older people have weak bladders? Not this guy, it seems.

I walk to his side and this time, he barely flinches. I remove his gag and throw it to the ground with disgust. Human saliva. So useless, they don't even use it to make their fur shiny.

"Water," he rasps.

I shoot him a glare. He dares to demand something from me? But he's lucky, there are a pitcher and a glass on his bedside table. I wouldn't have left the room for that, but since it's right in front of me, I pour him some water and hold it to his lips.

He spills more than he swallows, but he doesn't complain. Good boy. I wouldn't be happy if he did.

When he's finished, he looks at me with renewed interest. Most of the fear has disappeared and he seems a little more alert.

"You could have just asked," he mutters with a hoarse, brittle voice.

"What?"

"You could have asked. I would have let you stay here. There was no need to tie me up. Let alone almost kill me."

Huh. I don't quite know what to say to that. I didn't expect that in the slightest.

"Why would you have done that?"

He raises his eyebrows and stares at me. "You've not experienced much kindness in your life, have you, child? Two girls needing a bed for the night, of course I would have let you in. I would have even cooked you a hot meal. Did you grab some food from the pantry?"

I nod, still speechless.

"Good. Take some for the road. I'm not going to ask why you're here or what you're running from, but I heard the other girl's voice. She sounds young. Is she your sister?"

I finally find my voice again. "None of your business."

"Don't worry, not going to tell anyone you were here. I've got enough trouble with the police as it is. They took my cattle last time I complained about their corruption. Now I've got nothing left."

I don't have the time nor energy to pity him.

"Are those my trousers?"

He nods towards my new clothes.

"I hope you don't want them back."

"No, keep them. But if you climb up to the attic, you'll find some more suitable ones. I've got two chests full of women's clothes that you can help yourself to. It's not like Margaret still needs them."

"Your wife?" I can't help my curiosity.

"Daughter. Young farmhand came here when she was sixteen. Two months later, they left. Never saw her again. They sent me her wedding ring after she died in childbirth. Turns out her husband was involved in shady business. Had too many debts to count and couldn't afford a doctor when my daughter's labour turned awry. One day, destiny will get that bastard."

"I hope it does."

"Will you untie me now? I could make you breakfast. They took my cows, but I still have chickens that lay way too many eggs for me to eat all by myself."

I remember smelling those chickens yesterday. I have to admit, I was tempted to slaughter one, preferably while shifted, but an omelette sounds good too.

"If you run or try to call for help, I'll kill you," I warn him.

He grins slightly, exposing several missing teeth. "I have no doubts about that."

I UNDERESTIMATED HIM. CONSIDERING THE STATE OF HIS kitchen, he does make excellent scrambled eggs. I don't let him out of my sight, still wary of this supposedly good samaritan. People don't just help others, especially not after having been suffocated, tied up and gagged all night. I keep expecting him to run to the phone and call the police, or worse, some sirens he might know. Most humans are unaware of their presence - hell, even I didn't know about them until the Kindler case - but this close to Parseldon it might be different. I bet most politicians and rich people living there are sirens.

I have Sophie watch him while I explore the attic. His daughter was about my size, but there are some smaller clothes too, probably from when she was a child. No idea why he kept them, but it's good for us. As a farm girl, Margaret has mostly practical outfits and I can't help but purr when I find a pair of leather tights just like the ones I like to wear. Paired with a checkered shirt and some worn but comfortable boots, I could pass for a local peasant. I even find a straw hat for Sophie that might help cover her eye at least a little. It's not sunny or warm enough to warrant wearing such a hat, but she's a child and people might think she insisted on it while throwing a tantrum. I choose some loose trousers and a simple shirt for her, that way she won't stand out with her current expensive clothes.

Back downstairs, Sophie has joined the old man at the kitchen table and watches him curiously. Neither of the two is talking, but they seem to be comfortable in each other's presence. Weirdos. I watch them from the doorway, strangely touched by the image of the young girl and the old man sitting opposite each other. I don't feel guilty about what I did to him. I couldn't have known that he'd let us stay here voluntarily. Even now, I still have doubts. Once we leave this place, we're going to have to lay some false trails, just in case he reports us after all. It will take some time, but thanks to our shared nightmare, we're off to an early start.

Sophie's face is bruised, but she no longer presses the frozen peas against her eye. The bloody cloth lies discarded on the table.

"Do you have any sunglasses?" I ask and the man jumps. Sophie doesn't even flick an eyelid. Of course, she knew I was there. Her senses are well-trained, despite her never having been on a proper hunt.

"I may have an old pair lying around somewhere. I don't use them anymore; my eyesight is bad enough already without making it any darker. Why? I doubt it'll be very sunny today. The forecast says rain."

I nod towards Sophie and understanding spreads across his lined face.

"Of course. I'll see if I can find them."

I follow him, watching his every move as he sorts through several drawers until he finally finds a pair of old-fashioned sunglasses. They'll look ridiculous on Sophie, but hopefully, people will think she's blind and won't give her another look. One thing we learned back at the Pack. Disabled children are either stared at or ignored. And if they stare at her, they're going to see a poor farmer's girl who can't afford pretty clothes and not even glasses in the right size.

With this latest addition to our attire, we're ready to leave. Our backpack is full of supplies, although we hopefully won't need them if we meet Gryphon tonight. Still, better safe than sorry. The old man gazes at his backpack and looks as if he's about to say something, but then decides otherwise. Lucky. I wouldn't have taken kindly to him wanting it back. He's lucky that he's no longer tied up. For a moment, I debate to tie his hands enough that it will take him a few hours to get free, but Sophie takes my hand and looks at me with excitement.

"We're going to meet Gryphon."

I look down at her and return her smile. "Yes, we will. Are you ready to run?"

She nods. Bruising shows beneath her dark sunglasses, but nobody would think that she lost an eye overnight, albeit a mechanical one.

I shoulder the backpack and give the old guy one last look.

"If you rat us out, I'm going to come back and kill you."

He smiles. "Safe travels."

CHAPTER TWELVE

At first, we head North, leaving very obvious footprints in the muddy fields. Dawn is only just breaking over the horizon, but thick clouds hide most of the tentative sun rays trying to start the day. The air smells of rain even though the first drops haven't touched the ground yet. It's only a matter of minutes though before the clouds will release their heavy load.

After half an hour, we get to a small stream, only a foot deep and not flowing very fast. Perfect.

"Take off your shoes," I tell Sophie while pulling off my boots. She does so without questioning me.

The water is freezing, dispelling the last remnants of tiredness. I didn't get enough sleep, but I doubt I'll get much more tonight, not if we meet Gryphon. The two of us have a lot of catching up to do. Without Sophie and preferably in a bedroom.

We wade in the icy water until I'm sure that we've confused any potential pursuers enough. I'm glad we brought the blanket; it makes for an excellent towel. Wet feet are a sure way to get blisters. Back in our boots, we finally head West, across fields and even more fields. The landscape is so boring that I almost fall asleep while walking.

Sophie is quiet today. She's not asked a single question, which worries me a little. She was the complete opposite yesterday.

"Does your eye hurt?" I ask after an hour of silence.

"It's fine."

"That's not what I asked."

She scoffs. "A little, but it doesn't matter. It's healed too much to put the eye back in."

I stop in my tracks and turn around to her. "Why the fuck would you want to put it back in?"

She opens her hand and shows me the mechanical eye. She must have been carrying it the whole time. I thought she'd throw it away after all it's done to her, but instead, she not only kept it, but she's now looking at her with a certain longing. Silly girl.

"I can't see," she replies almost defiantly. "And it could make me see properly again. I'll never get my sight back. You can't grow me a new eye. So now I'm stuck with one and I don't like it."

I wouldn't be surprised if she stamped her foot and threw a major temper tantrum. She's close to it, I'm sure. But this isn't the time nor place, no matter how traumatising it all must be for her.

"Did you like being hurt? Did you like being controlled? Did you like them forcing to hurt other people? No? Then don't complain. I know it's awful but it's better than before."

"It's not your eye that's missing," she snaps. "You've still got both of yours. Maybe I should scratch one of yours out so you know what it's like."

Wow, that escalated quickly. I'd love to get into a long

argument with her, but we can't linger. Lord Delaney's grunts could be following us. We need to get to the inn and Gryphon as soon as possible.

"Maybe there are ways to help you," I say as calmly as I can. "When we're in Attenburgh, we can take you to see a doctor. And tonight, Gryphon can take a look at you. I told you that he studied medicine, right?"

Her scowl lessens a little. "Do you really think they can make me see again?"

I try to believe that it's possible. I don't want her to pick up on the doubt I have, so I convince myself with all the mental force I can muster.

"There are some very intelligent scientists and doctors out there. And we already know that mechanical eyes exist. Maybe we can have one like that made for you, but this time just for you, with nobody able to watch what you see or control you in any way. We'll find a way to make you better, I promise. We just need to get home first. Then we can deal with all of that. Alright?"

Her gaze wanders over my face as if she's trying to see if I'm lying. I can usually smell lies when spoken by a human, although it's harder but not impossible for shifters. I'll definitely teach her that skill when we're home. I have so much to pass on to her. So much training that she missed out on. Luckily, she'll have Ryker to teach her everything there's to know about being a cat. There's no better authority than him, having lived as a cat for all his life.

"Alright." She gives me a small smile. "But if you lied, I'll scratch out both of your eyes."

"Deal. Now let's continue, we don't want to be late to your appointment with Doctor Gryphon."

To my surprise, she takes my hand. Hers is small in mine, reminding me of how young she is. She doesn't behave like it, most of the time, but I do have to be mindful of it. She's not as strong as she makes out to be.

We continue our walk in silence, but it's a comfortable silence. In my mind, I'm trying to figure out what I'm going to say to Gryphon once we finally meet again. Do I start with 'hello'? Is that enough? Or do I simply grab him and kiss him? Or will it be strange to see him again after all this time? Will there still be chemistry between us?

My foot sinks into a hole in the ground and I almost stumble. Fucking rabbits, leaving holes all over the place. Teaches me to have my head in the clouds. I need to focus both on our surroundings and on potential enemies. We're not safe yet, no matter how much I want to believe that. Until we're back in Attenburgh, I can't let my guard down. And even then...

I sigh when I realise the truth. As long as Delaney or any other sirens are still out there, I'll never be safe. Neither will be my family.

Once I'm back home, we'll have to make plans. No more hiding. No more defending. It's time to go on the offensive and get rid of them once and for all.

THE RIVER IS BIGGER THAN I IMAGINED. IT'S SO BROAD that it feels more like a lake than a river. The current is strong; too strong to attempt to swim to the other side. Not that I ever planned to do that. We'll use the bridge just like Gryphon said.

We take a quick break to have a drink and open one of the cans of corned beef we took from the old man's pantry, before continuing our trek. Sophie is still quiet but she seems to be deep in thought rather than angry at me. I let her be. She'll talk when she's ready.

We must be further downstream than I'd hoped. After hours of running and walking, there's still no sign of the bridge. I'm starting to worry that we may have been going the wrong direction. Maybe we should have turned left rather than right when we reached the river. Gryphon didn't know where exactly we were so maybe he got it wrong?

There's no choice but continuing along the river though. About an hour ago, the wilderness gave way to a rough track that has made our progress a lot faster. It will also hide our footprints from anyone looking for us. Many people have walked along here; the most recent scents are barely a few hours old. If we continue running, we might even overtake them, but I don't want to exert too much energy. We may have to fight before night falls, who knows, so we walk at a brisk pace rather than run. I wish we could shift; we'd cover much more ground that way, but it's too risky. I don't know what will happen if I ask Sophie to shift. She might turn feral and that would waste more time than walking as humans.

I'm tempted to shift and let her ride on me though. Nobody has ever done that before. I'm not a horse. But she's my little sister and her exhaustion is starting to show. I doubt she ever had to do anything like this before. Almost no sleep, losing her eye and running for two days straight...yup, it's no surprise she's getting slower.

"Let me know if you want another break," I tell her at some point, but she ignores me. She actually increases her pace as if to prove me wrong. Good girl. I smile but don't comment on it.

Slowly, the river is getting narrower. It looks more like a river than a lake now, but at the same time, the current increases. White foam lines the muddy banks, covering stones smooth from the water's embrace.

A sound breaks through the silence and I stop, holding up my hand to alert Sophie. She gives me a small nod. She's heard it too. The snap of a twig, caused by something heavy. Too big to be an animal unless maybe a bear - and none of those live in these parts of the world, as far as I know.

I crouch on the ground and motion Sophie to do the same. Long grass grows on either side of us and should hide us from view. I strain my senses to find out who made the sound. Male voices drift on the wind, too far to understand their words. It could be grunts searching for us or simple travellers. As much as I hope for the latter, I can't risk it.

As quietly as I can, I take off my backpack and pull some of the knives from it. I already have the axe slung in a sheath around my waist, but I'm more used to knives and prefer the way they can be used for both throwing and stabbing. And slicing. And nipping. And torturing. And threatening. That's why I love them. I could try and throw the axe, but I've never done that before. It should mostly work as a deterrent. Look at my wicked, sharp axe and run away before I behead you. Something like that.

Sophie takes a knife as well. She holds it awkwardly. I'm worried she might hurt herself more than others, but I leave her be. Holding a weapon will hopefully make her feel safer. I can scent her fear. She's trying to be brave though and I won't let her notice that I know how scared she is.

We stay like that, waiting for them to either come closer or to disappear. Sadly, they are following the same track we're on. We could hide in the grass, but to be honest, I'm tired of hiding. There are only two men. I should be able to handle them. I'm not back to full strength, but I've got weapons and I'm desperate.

Desperation makes the best motivator. Always fear those who're desperate enough to take risks.

Finally, their voices are audible.

"...sweet. Can't wait to taste her."

"What master doesn't know doesn't hurt him."

"He only wants the young one unharmed. We can knock her out and have fun with the older one."

"She smells delicious. Pity he didn't let us enjoy her at the house."

I shudder. Definitely not random travellers. I look at Sophie to check if she listened too. Her wide-eyed stare tells me everything I need to know.

"We're going to be fine," I whisper. "Hide in the grass. I'll deal with them."

She shakes her head. "I'll fight."

CHAPTER THIRTEEN

The anticipation before a kill is often better than the actual fight. Adrenaline rushes through me, reminding me of the good old days. I'm about to take a life. Two, in fact. Without any regrets or moral implications. Wonderful. It's just what I needed. True, it would be even better if I was in top shape and not half-starved, but you can't have it all.

I've persuaded Sophie to hide in the high grass after all with the promise that this will make it easier for her to surprise them. I hope she'll decide differently and will stay hidden, but she's my sister. I doubt she'll back down.

I stay in place, crouched but ready. I'm not going to hide. I'll confront them head-on. Today, I'm not an assassin. I'm a warrior ready to take revenge. My mates would tell me off for this. So would Lily. But I need a bit of fun, and taking risks is a lot of fun. They'll never have to know. Besides, I'm their boss. I'm still the head of M.E.O.W., even though I took a long and involuntary leave of absence. I hope they kept the company going. We'd just started to make a name for ourselves in Attenburgh, especially with Lady Lara, the mayor, on our side.

The two men are now so close that I can smell them. They're both mutants, but there's a surprising amount of human left in their scents. So far, most of the grunts I've encountered weren't very bright, but these two had an actual conversation. Maybe they were created to be more intelligent than the others. That makes them more dangerous, but they're cocky and way too confident that they'll catch us. And I know that they're intending to hurt me, probably kill me. That makes it all the more motivating to kill them first. And hopefully make them suffer a little, too. Kill one, torture the other. That's the plan.

When they're around fifty metres away, I get up, revealing myself to them. They don't seem surprised in the slightest. Their senses are better than those of humans, much better. I hope they experience pain like humans, though. It would be no fun otherwise.

I twirl my knives in my hands. They're kitchen knives, nowhere as sharp and well balanced as the ones I'm used to, but they'll do. In the right hands, even a blunt knife is a formidable weapon. And my hands are the best. Trained from childhood to kill.

I grin at them. My prey is coming to me. I don't even have to hunt it.

One of them pulls a long sword from his back. The blade is ragged on one end, like a breadknife. How ugly. The other man has two curved swords, similar to a set I bought at an auction. I didn't like them as much as I'd thought, so they now hang on my wall as decoration.

"If you give up now, we'll knock you out and you can sleep all the way back to the master," one of them shouts. "If you don't, it'll hurt."

I give them a sweet smile. "If you give up now, I'll hurt you anyway."

They both flash their teeth in feral grins. They're going to enjoy this just as much as I will. I'm almost glad. They'll die happy men.

Without warning, they both start running at me. My instincts kick in and suddenly it's just like before. My body moves in one fluid motion as I jump out of the way while at the same time throwing on of the knives at the mutant on the left. He dodges incredibly fast, but it still hits him in the shoulder. He grunts as it embeds itself in his flesh but he doesn't slow down. He rips it out while running, making blood squirt from the wound. What an idiot.

Then they're upon me and I lose track of who I'm cutting and who's bleeding the most. The annoying thing is that those mutants heal almost as fast as I injure them. Their healing abilities are much better than mine, which means I have to be careful not to let them hurt me. Which isn't easy, considering there's two of them and one of me. They're massive and they're well-trained, wielding their weapons like extensions of their bodies. I'm kind of impressed; I didn't expect them to use anything but brute force. They work well together. Again, I respect them for it. Still, I'm not going to let them win.

While they both swing their swords at me, I let myself drop flat to the ground and cut across their hamstrings. They howl in pain and the one to my right wavers, clearly having trouble staying upright. I put all my weight on my arms and swirl my legs around, kicking him right where I cut him.

He goes down on his knees, but the other guy is still standing - and he's pissed. His sword whistles through the air and I just about manage to evade him. Almost. The tip of his sword has cut into my cheek, but it's not a deep wound and it doesn't hurt enough to distract me. I jump back to my feet and then onto the kneeling man's shoulders. He topples over, giving me the chance to swipe my knives at his throat. He's too fast though and manages to get his arm in the way. The blades slice through his flesh until they meet bone, but they're not sharp enough to cut through that. Blood streams from his wounds, but annoyingly, he's still alive.

The other man doesn't wait for me to correct that error. He tackles me from behind and it's only thanks to my well-oiled reflexes that he doesn't cleave me in half. I jump off the other guy and face sword-man. The grin on his face mirrors my own. We're both enjoying this. The adrenaline rushing through my body is like rolling in catnip, sweet and addictive.

"Watch out!" Sophie suddenly yells, but it's too late. One of the curved swords cuts though my left arse cheek. He must have missed whatever his target was, but it hurts like hell. I won't be sitting at the inn tonight.

I growl and increase my pace, duelling with both men at once. My left leg is a little numb, making it harder to move quickly. I'm starting to feel like I'm at a disadvantage. They heal too fast. If I want to end this before I get any more wounds, I'll have to cut off their heads like I've done with mutants in the past. I doubt my knives will be sharp enough for that, so I let one of them fall to the ground and draw the axe from my sheath.

The weight of it means my attacks aren't as well balanced, but I have more reach. Axes won't become my favourite weapon any time soon, but I have to admit that burying the blade in one of the grunts' chest is very satisfying. He howls like a wolf and stares at the axe embedded between his ribs. Then he grins and grabs the hilt, forcing me to let go of it. He rips it from his flesh and

I watch in shock as the wound knits itself together. Fuck. Now he has my axe and I'm one dagger short.

I think it's time to switch tactics. In some fights, I can use my small size to an advantage, but right now, it makes it harder for me. I need to be bigger.

I drop the second knife and shift before it even hits the ground.

Fur erupts from my skin as my body changes shape; the best feeling in the world. Besides bathing in catnip. My fingernails turn into claws and I swipe at the closest grunt while they're not quite ready yet. They cut through his skin like butter, smooth and satisfying.

The smell of blood hits me and my cat pushes to the surface. She takes over and I let her. She's been cooped up for too long and deserves to play with her prey. The grunts seem clueless about how to fight a panther. They were good at duelling me, but now I've got the upper hand.

I launch myself into the air and land on one of them, toppling him over before he can even raise his sword. My jaws clamp around his throat and my teeth sink into his neck. A satisfying crunch signals the breaking of his spine. I turn my head from side to side, then pull, until I've got his throat ripped out, leaving a bloody mess in front of me.

Blood fills my mouth and I swallow it. Pleasure shoots through my body, my mind, my soul. New strength makes my muscles ripple and my fur rise. I'm strong. And I need more of this sweet nectar.

The other mutant shouts a battle cry and launches himself at me. I swat him away. He won't distract me from my meal. I lick up the blood still pouring from the man's open throat. It's warm, like tea, but heady like expensive red wine. I can't get enough of it.

I drink and drink, and even when pain shoots through my back, I ignore it. I already feel the wound healing; the process fastened by the power of the blood I'm devouring. I'm invincible. I'm stronger than ever before. And I'm going to squeeze the life out of the man trying to hurt me.

I swirl around and meet him head-on, easily evading his strike. I may be big, but I'm also fast and agile. I swipe my claws over his stomach, leaving deep gashes. His entrails peek out from inside. Tasty. I want to eat them. Slurp them like spaghetti.

He clutches his belly with one hand, but he's not done fighting. And he's angry. No, furious. He knows he might die and that means he's desperate. He's got nothing to lose. And that's how he fights. Wild, untamed, reckless. I love it. But I love the scent of his blood even more. I want it. Mix it with that of his friend and enjoy the cocktail.

I no longer want to play. I'm hungry. I go in for the kill, not caring that his sword cuts through some of the tendons in my left front leg. I lose my balance, but it's too late for him. His throat is ripped out before he can scream. His eyes are wide, staring at me in shock, then the lights go out and his spirit fades. I let his lifeless body drop to the ground and begin to feast.

I prefer lapping up the blood, but I don't mind the little pieces of meat that mix with it. Protein, right? It's good for you.

"Kat, stop it!"

I ignore my little sister's shout. She doesn't know how good this feels. I've been starved, not just as a human, but as a cat, too. I need this. Need the energy that flows from the mutants' blood into my body. I purr in contentment. This is heaven. I could imagine cat heaven to be like that, if such a thing exists. Fountains, no, waterfalls of mutant blood. Catnip trees reaching towards the sky. Cat milk - the stuff humans give to kittens - in large ponds. Panther-sized toys filled with catnip and silver vine. And to top it off, some small cardboard boxes I can try to squeeze myself into.

Without thinking, I drop to one side and rub against the grassy ground. Sooooo good. I want someone to scratch between my ears. Hard. But since nobody is doing that, I push against one of the grunts' bodies and use him as a scratch tree. Yes, rub that pussy.

With every drop of blood I lap up, my cat becomes stronger while my human self shrinks into the background. Rational thought doesn't matter when there are mutant blood and meat to enjoy. The pleasure of sating my hunger is the only thing that matters.

Once I've finally had my fill, I stretch my long limbs and yawn. Time for a nap. But not here. It's too exposed and there's a pesky human trying to get my attention. I ignore her. I'm no longer hungry and besides, she's not fleshy enough to make a good dessert.

I shake my fur, getting rid of some of the blood, and run away from the river. Shouts follow me, but I'm far more interested in the forest in the distance. I'll find a tree there and have a long, relaxing nap. And then it'll be time to hunt. Now that I've tasted mutant blood, I need more of it. I can't imagine going back to eating small mammals. No way. And if I can't get any mutants, I'll have to resort to humans.

CHAPTER FOURTEEN

Life as a cat is easy. Sleep, eat, sleep, repeat.

The forest is full of life. I do eat the occasional squirrel, but I long for something more satisfying. I've been back to where I killed the mutants, but they'd disappeared. I'd even licked the ground where they'd lain, hoping for some of that sweet, alluring taste. No such luck.

The human within me knows where more mutants are, but she hides that knowledge from me. She's refusing to talk to me, so I've pushed her away, locked her deep inside me. I used to be the prisoner within her; now we've changed roles.

I love my freedom. Humans are so complicated. It makes me bored just thinking about all their problems. I should have taken control a long time ago. It's better for both of us. In this forest, we're the biggest animal around. Everyone cowers before us. Everyone is dinner.

I jump off the branch I've been resting on and rub against the bark of the tree. So good. It's not the same as being stroked by a human, but it's still pleasant enough.

I'm hungry, but I'm not in the mood for squirrel. I need a proper meal.

I push into my mind until I reach Kat. She glares at me. She's not happy about being kept in the dark. I give her a little purr, almost an apology but not quite.

Where do I find more yummy mutants?

She pushes up her mental barriers and I'm expelled. I growl. That wasn't very polite. I only wanted to know where to get more of the best food around. She must feel my hunger. When she's in charge, I feel her desires too. They're not high on my list of priorities - I much prefer to snooze and let the world drift by until she lets me shift - but I do know what her hunger feels like. Maybe I should starve myself until she tells me her secret, but that sounds like too much work.

Maybe it's time to leave the forest and look for the nearest human settlement. I might find mutants there, and if not, humans don't taste too bad either. Kat has never let me eat one, but I've had their blood and meat in my mouth while killing them. It'll be a change from squirrel and deer. More fun to hunt, too. Humans are slow and don't have any claws or even hooves to defend themselves with, but they are fairly clever. They create weapons and aren't hesitant to use them. They're inherently cruel. Especially when it comes to their own kind. Some of the things I've seen through Kat's eyes have made me very glad that I'm not human.

I shake my fur once again and turn towards the fresh scent of the river. Humans, here I come.

🐾 🐾 🐾

I'M A CAPTIVE. AGAIN. IF IT WASN'T SO DEPRESSING, I'D laugh. Imprisoned by my cat side. She's taken over like never before. Is that what they call going feral? It must be. Lennox went feral when his collar was first removed, but he didn't stay a wolf for as long as I have now been running around as a panther. Five days. I'm so sick of the taste of squirrel. I'll become a vegetarian after this. Or at least I'll stick to animals that have more meat and less sinew. And a lot less furry. I think there's still squirrel hair lining my throat. That's going to be one epic hairball.

I can do nothing but watch as my cat runs towards the river where I killed the grunts. We've been here before, but this time, she turns right and follows the path upstream. I hope Sophie made it to the inn and found Gryphon. I was so close. But of course it wasn't to be. A little bit of luck would have been too much of a change to all the misery that's befallen me. I didn't expect my cat to be the traitor though.

She's unpredictable in her frenzied state. I don't think I'd be able to stop her from killing any humans she might come across. And that's bad. She'll be caught; news will get to Lord Delaney and he'll send more mutants. She'd love that, but I know better. The delicious taste of grunt blood isn't worth the risk of ending up in Delaney's dungeon again. That would be worse than being kept prisoner by my own cat. Who's kind of me. So I'm basically being kept hostage by me. My life is crazy.

We come across more and more human scents. The bridge and inn must be close. I gather my energy, ready to attack and try to take over from my cat. I won't be responsible for her killing humans. I've got the monopoly on that, and I only do it for money. Not for food.

By the time the bridge comes into view - a large white monstrosity wide enough to let several carts pass next to each other - I'm almost ready. By sitting still and letting her take full control, I've been able to conserve energy. I'm stronger now than when she surprised and overwhelmed me during the battle. I can do this. I just need to wait for a moment when she's distracted.

Dusk is creeping over the flat landscape. Hopefully, that will keep us from being spotted. A massive panther running across a bridge will draw attention.

We never make it to the bridge though. A new scent hits our nostrils and my cat stops to sniff the air. It's a familiar scent; no, two of them. We recognise them at the same time. A cat and a wolf. Ryker and Lennox. They're here. I kind of want to cry in relief. They'll stop her from doing something I'll regret.

My cat's thoughts are easy to read. She's conflicted. Does she want to meet her friends? Or is her hunger more important? I'm glad she considers them friends. I wasn't quite sure about that, not after realising that every time I'd shifted in the past, it was still mostly me in the driving seat. She had control over our body, but I was still able to steer our direction and decisions. Maybe our feelings too, including who we consider friend and foe.

Let's meet Lennox and Ryker, I tell her but immediately realise my mistake.

She's a cat. She'll do exactly the opposite of what she's told. I groan in frustration when she continues running towards the bridge rather than follow my mates' scents which sway to the left, away from the river. Stupid cat.

No catnip for you ever again.

She doesn't deign me with a reply. I hate her.

⁎ ⁎ ⁎ ⁎ ⁎ ⁎

MY HUNGER IS INCREASING. SALIVA DRIPS FROM MY MOUTH while I run towards my dinner. The smell of humans is getting stronger. Fleshy, delicious humans, so full of blood that is just waiting to be lapped up. A few carts are rolling over the bridge. Should I attack the first one I come across or should I go to the house that will be full of humans, their stomachs full with food that I might enjoy too? It's basically like one of the sausages Kat enjoys.

A noise from my left makes me slow down and look around for threats. Two shapes in the distance. The wind carries their scents to me. Kat's mates. I'd hoped they'd be further away, but they're running towards me. They know I'm here. No, they're not going to take my dinner from me.

I ignore them and run faster. The bridge is so close. The human scents are getting more distinguishable. A family is on the cart closest to me, two adults and a child. I'll ignore the child; it's not got enough meat on its bones to be a satisfying meal. The adults, however, are large and fatty, the female in particular. If she's not enough, the male will be dessert. He smells older and might not be as tasty. We'll see.

My stomach growls. Almost there.

A wolf's howl breaks through the silence. The humans look up and speed up their carts, forcing their horses to run. I growl in irritation. He's done that on purpose. I should punish him for that. Yes, I think I will. My dinner won't get far. I'm faster than any idiot horse. The anticipation will make my feast even more satisfying.

I turn and run towards the wolf. Ryker is nowhere to be seen but I'm sure he's nearby. Those two males need to be taught a lesson. Never get between a cat and her dinner. My claws shoot from my paws as I think of scratching them. I don't want to kill them, just injure them enough that they'll remember.

His scent hits me before his claws do. I hesitate. He smells like a friend. Like my mate.

My hesitation costs me. Within an instant, I'm on the

ground and his teeth are pressed tight against my throat. He howls with his jaws around my neck, almost shattering my sensitive eardrums.

I'm torn. I want to fight him. I don't like being under his control. But his scent...I want to roll in it. Rub against him. Lick him all over. He may be a wolf but he smells like home. All my thoughts about dinner dissolve into thin air.

Mate.

The howl is answered by a loud meow in the distance. Ryker is coming. My heart beats even faster.

Mate.

Lennox releases his pressure on my throat a little, clearly realising that I'm not about to tear him to pieces. He yelps and his tongue shoots out, stroking my fur.

Kat stirs deep within me. She wants to feel that touch too. I push her away. This is my moment. It's not just her who's missed them. She may love them, but they're my mates. That's so much more intense than human love.

A purr breaks from my chest when I smell Ryker. While Lennox is exotic, Ryker is home. He's a cat like me, even though he looks more like a house cat than a panther. We share the same mentality.

By the time he reaches us, I've turned into a purring mess. Lennox steps back, sensing that it's no longer necessary to keep me restrained. Holy catnip, I'd get myself chained up if it meant being with these two males.

"Hey," Ryker meows and nuzzles my cheek.

"Hey."

I don't have words for more than that. My brain is in shock. My heart is about to implode. Suddenly, everything is perfect again. The sun may have disappeared behind the hills in the distance, but to me, it feels like it's shining bright right above us. Warmth spreads through my entire body.

"Shift," he says and gives me an encouraging nudge. "I

want to touch you properly. So does Lennox and he can't understand you like this."

My purring immediately stops and I growl. I'm not giving way to Kat. If we shift, she'll be in charge. I won't have that.

"No," I hiss. "I'll stay like this. She's made a mess of things and I'm not going to give her control again."

"Oh, Kat," he meows softly. His voice is milk with catnip syrup, oh so delicious and sweet. "You're one and the same. You told me once, remember? It sometimes feels like you're a cat and a human trapped in the same body, but you're really the same being. Two sides of your personality. Did they force you to split? What did they do to you?"

"We're not the same," I growl. "She's weak. She needed to be stopped."

"You're not weak. You're the strongest woman I know. I don't know what happened to you, but we'll fix it. Just shift and we'll talk properly about it, okay? Gryphon is nearby, together with your sister. We can join them and we'll catch up. There's so much to talk about."

I'm not in the mood for talking. I want to take him, now. And Lennox. I want to fuck them. Mark them as mine. Make sure they know they're my mates.

Lennox hasn't been able to follow our conversation, but he seems to realise my distress. He lies on the ground next to me and gently strokes my side with one paw. My purring starts again, out of control.

Kat nudges me from inside. She wants out. She wants to get naked.

Are we truly the same? It doesn't feel that way. I dimly remember being part of her, but not anymore. She's locked away and I want to keep her that way. I'm the stronger one. I'm the one with the claws and the muscles. She's a weak, puny human who has to use knives instead of claws. It's pitiful, really.

Ryker sighs and steps back. His scent is still driving me crazy. I can't have him walk away from me. I need him. Before I can get up and lick him, he shifts. He's become good at it. It's fluid and quick. Like he's done it all his life.

He's gloriously naked. Even though I found him sexier while he was still a cat, I can't help but appreciate his physique. His chest is chiselled, his abs ready to draw my claws across, his cock...

Kat is becoming stronger. She's pushing against me. When did she become this strong? It's getting harder to keep her out.

"Kat, shift. I need to see you."

His voice is hoarse with need. Mine would be the same but I don't find any words. My mind is in turmoil. Do I shift? Do I stay a cat like I should? It's my natural form. I should have sex like this. It doesn't matter that Lennox is a wolf. He's the right size and he shouldn't find it too hard. It's just a case of pushing his cock into me. The species doesn't matter, it's not like I want to become pregnant.

"Kat."

He's impatient. His cock is hard. He wants me just like I want him.

I turn to look at Lennox. His eyes are burning with desire. He gives me one last pat on my fur, then gets up to all fours and shifts. Now I have two naked human males to stare at. But still, I'm refusing to shift.

Kat is throwing a tantrum, shouting all sorts of obscenities at me, but she's not quite strong enough to break through. I'd have to give her permission. And there's no way I'm going to do that. They're mine. She can fuck off and sulk. She's great at sulking. It's always annoyed me.

"Please," Lennox says. It's the first time I've heard his

voice in months and it almost breaks me. Has he always sounded this alluring? Gryphon is the siren, not Lennox, yet it feels like he's wrapped some magic around me with his voice alone.

My purring betrays me, growing ever louder. They know how much I want them. They're counting on it. They think that if they can tempt me enough, I'm going to shift. But no. I can't. I won't. Kat is too weak to deal with what's to come. She thinks everything will be fine once we get home. I know better. Our enemies won't just give up. They'll come for us. They'll hunt us down no matter where we go. She's not ready to accept that yet and that makes her weak. She needs me to stay in charge. She may not understand that now, but she will once we go into battle again. We'll have to fight soon. There's no way around it. Running won't save us.

Lennox joins Ryker in presenting his body. He even rubs his cock, as if to taunt me. Evil males. Drool runs down my chin. I don't think I could purr any louder. Why can't they just shift back so I can take them? I won't touch them as humans, that would be icky. I think the only reason I find them sexy now is because Kat's desire is echoing through me. I don't find humans attractive, but she does.

"Kat, shift," Ryker commands impatiently. "I'm not going to last like this for much longer."

The hunger in his eyes is all-encompassing.

I can't resist it.

I give in and let Kat dive to the surface.

Goodbye, my mates. Look after her.

CHAPTER FIFTEEN

It's like resurfacing from a lucid dream that I had no control over. I blink at the two men staring at me. Then look down at me. I'm naked, just like they are. It's strange being human again. I stretch my limbs, enjoying the feeling of not having fur. I usually prefer my cat body, but having been forced to be in it for several days at once has made me appreciate my human form. I mean...boobs.

"Kat," Ryker gasps, and then they're upon me. He claims my mouth while Lennox hugs me from behind, his hands exploring my skin as if it's the first time he's touched me. I lean into their embrace and let go of all the memories, all the worries, everything that's happened. I brush it all away and just focus on the moment. Ryker's taste. Lennox's touch. Their scents that make the air sparkle.

I can't help but moan at the sensations. I'd be purring, but this deep, sensual moan is almost as good.

Ryker swipes his tongue against mine while his yellow eyes burn into my soul. I close my eyes. I don't want him to see inside of me. He wouldn't like what he finds in there.

I've changed so much since we last saw each other. Let's leave all that for later. Now, I just want to be with them. Become one with them.

Lennox cups my breasts and squeezes them gently. Again, I moan. I want more. He rolls my nipples between his fingers, elongating them in a way that drives me crazy. And he knows that. He's counting on it. His cock is hard against my back, while Ryker's pushes against my stomach. I reach down, twisting a little so I can embrace both of them. Groans fill the quiet evening air.

Without breaking the kiss, Ryker pushes a finger into me. I almost come from that alone. And when he gently rubs my clit, I fall apart. I cry out as my legs give out, but they've got me in their arms, holding me, carrying me through the storm and into the next wave. One of them pushes into me while the other touches me all over. I lose track of who does what. I don't care. We're all one, together, three beings turned into one flame of desire. One is missing, stopping us from becoming the bonfire we're meant to be, but I can't focus on that. The moment is what matters.

"Kat," Lennox groans. I think he's the one inside of me, pushing in with hard and fast strokes. Ryker sucks on my nipples, sending lightning bolts deep into my core. I'm close to coming again. And again.

We end up on the muddy ground, our skin covered in dirt, but that doesn't matter. We merge, we come together, we groan, we kiss, we love.

Time becomes meaningless. I don't know how often they make me come. How often they come inside me. How often we kiss.

It's perfect.

I feel alive again. Until now, I hadn't realised how much I'd shut off my emotions, but now they're bare. I'm vulnerable but I'm not afraid. I know my mates are there for me. Just like I'll always be there for them.

*　*　*　*　*　*

THE STARS ARE OUR BLANKET AS WE LIE ON THE GRASS, THE guys on either side of me. Our hands are entwined and I have no intention of letting go of them anytime soon. I need their touch, the connection with them. It still doesn't quite feel real. I'd almost given up hope that this moment would ever come. Together again. A family.

"Gryphon will be pissed," Lennox says into the silence. "I bet he thought he'd be the first."

"We'll repeat this," I mutter sleepily. "All four of us."

"I'm looking forward to it. Maybe we can have a bed next time? And a little less mud?"

I can't help but laugh. It breaks from me, laughter upon laughter, until I'm out of breath and my cheeks are burning.

"You okay?" Ryker asks, amusement lacing his voice.

"Never better."

"Good. That's exactly what I wanted to hear."

Lennox sighs. "We should probably head back. They'll be worried. We said we'd be back by nightfall."

"Gryphon and Sophie are in a cottage not far from the Inn you were supposed to meet at," Ryker explains. "We persuaded him to take on babysitting duties since the two of us can cover much more ground."

"How did you get here?" I ask.

"Lily phoned us as soon as she heard from you. She told us to stay put until Gryphon got to you, but neither of us listened. Lennox got here two days ago and I only arrived this morning." He chuckles. "We've seen quite a bit of the country in the past few months. Luckily neither of us was too far away."

"It felt like a lot longer than two days," Lennox sighs. "Gryphon had a vague idea where you were hiding out, but Sophie warned him that it would be too dangerous to seek you out on his own, while human. She wanted to shift and do it herself, but he didn't let her." He smirks. "The two of them have struck up quite the relationship."

"Relationship?"

"He's like an uncle to her already. I don't want to say father figure but-"

"Father figure," Ryker confirms with a grin. "He's got her eating out of his hand and vice versa. The two of them will be trouble, I promise you."

Interesting. I didn't expect that, but what do I know. Gryphon already has a sister, so it makes sense for him to know how to deal with a young girl, but I didn't think Sophie would easily trust anyone. It almost makes me a little jealous.

"Are the others still in Attenburgh?" I ask.

Lennox nods. "Lily and Bethany have been travelling around as well, searching for any whisper of you, but now they're back at home. Benjamin and Caitlin have been holding down the fort. Lady Lara has been helping a lot too. She's been providing us with leads, funds and the chance to travel with some of her employees to save us both time and money. She'll be so glad to hear that you've been found."

As grateful as I am for her help, being in her debt leaves a bitter taste in my mouth. "I'll pay her back."

Ryker chuckles. "She told me you'd say that. And she's planning to make you work for it. She's got a whole list of jobs waiting for you once you're back home. Although we've helped her too, done enquiries, delivered letters, that sort of stuff. We work quite well together."

It sounds like it. Lady Lara is one shrewd woman. And very intelligent, kind and gorgeous at the same time. I'm glad I've got her on my side. Having her as an enemy would be quite the challenge. I'm kind of looking forward to spending more time with her again. I was taken just when we'd started to get to know each other.

Lennox sits up and yawns loudly. "We better go. I doubt you'll want to shift again, which means we have quite a walk ahead of us."

He gets up, meaning I now have a dangling cock in front of my face. All sorts of naughty thoughts spring into my mind, but luckily, I'm still sated. And there's no time, I get that. I'm looking forward to a soft, warm bed, and before that, a long shower. I'll never take those two things for granted. It's strange how quickly I got used to these luxuries. When I grew up in the Pack, a shower consisted of standing under a cold garden hose in the courtyard. Our beds were flea-ridden and dirty. Yes, I've become spoilt. And I love it.

Together, we walk at a brisk pace towards the bridge. Luckily, no humans are around at this time of night, so we don't get any weird looks for being stark naked. Whenever I look at my two men, temptation grabs hold of me, but I always manage to get a grip.

Shower. Bed. Gryphon.

It becomes my mantra.

On the way, the guys tell me of all the places they visited while looking for me. I haven't even heard of half those towns and villages. In the beginning, they mostly searched on the other side of the country because that's where their leads indicated I was being held.

"Do you think Lord Delaney planted those rumours?" I ask when Lennox finishes his tale.

The wolf sucks in a sharp breath. "Lord Delaney? *The* Lord Delany? Is he the siren who held you?"

Ah. Yes. I've not told them anything about what happened to me. I've not felt strong enough to do so yet. And I only want to talk about it once, which means I won't do it until I've got all the important people gathered around me. The guys will just have to wait.

"Yes. What do you know about him?"

"He's only the most influential advisor to the Prime Minister. How have you not heard of him? He was never elected to any political role, but he's got more power than most career politicians. He whispers in the PM's ear and everything he wants is done. He has some kind of power over the Prime Minister that makes him untouchable. According to the rumours, anyway. I doubt anyone would be brave enough to accuse him of that directly."

I shrug. "You know I'm not interested in politics. But yes, he was the one who made me self-kidnap myself."

"Self-kidnap?" Ryker interrupts. "What the hell?"

"It was my choice. I walked into that cage. I wasn't taken. I chose to do it."

Ryker grips my shoulders and makes me turn to him until I'm staring right into his intense yellow eyes.

"He forced you. You didn't have a choice. He was threatening your little sister and of course you would never have let him hurt her. You were kidnapped, Kat. You didn't do it to yourself, if that's what you've been telling yourself."

Lennox hugs me from behind, turning this into a Kat sandwich. "Listen to him. You have no fault in what happened to you. Don't you dare blame yourself."

"I don't," I protest, but it's a lie. "I don't say that to put the fault on me. It made me get through it. It gave me control over the situation. Saying that I self-kidnapped puts the power in my hands. Do you understand?"

"I'm not sure I do," Ryker mutters. His eyes bore deep into mine as if he's trying to discern whether I'm telling the truth. I don't even know myself. If I did, then I didn't just lie to them, I also lied to myself. It's all a bit of a mess. My mind must be the most chaotic place on the planet just now.

Lennox runs his hands over my stomach in a strangely soothing motion. Not so soothing is the fact that his dick presses against my back, reminding me once again that all three of us are naked. Resist the temptation, kitty. No milk for you until later.

I untangle myself from the sandwich and continue walking, pointedly not looking back. Without a word, they join me, each reaching out to take my hands. I let them, and yes, I do enjoy the feeling, although I wouldn't admit that to them.

Together, we walk over the bridge. My feet sigh in relief at the change of terrain. The cobblestone is so much more comfortable to walk on than the uneven, muddy ground that's full of hidden rocks and sharp grass. My shifter healing is almost back to normal, but it still hurts.

We must make a curious sight. Three people, naked, strolling hand in hand over a bridge in the middle of the night. Luckily, there's nobody out to see us. The night is our friend and gently hides us from view until we get to the cottage where Gryphon is waiting for me.

CHAPTER SIXTEEN

He doesn't say anything. He simply pulls me against his chest and captures my mouth with his, kissing me like he needs it to survive. My tiredness disappears a little, enough to return his kiss with just as much passion. The other two guys disappear into the house, giving us some space. They've already had their turn. Gryphon is the one who's had to wait the longest. We'd been so close yet I never made it to him. Not until now.

I pour all my regret into the kiss. All the love I have for him. And he gives back as much as he takes. He makes me feel like I'm the only woman in the entire universe.

"Ew, get a room!"

Sophie has appeared behind him. Gryphon chuckles but doesn't end the kiss; in fact, he turns even wilder. He nips at my bottom lip, just the way I like it. No, not just *like*. Love. I'm on fire and he's the one stoking the flames.

"Where did your clothes go?" Sophie asks with the tone of an exasperated mother.

"Yes, where did your clothes go?" Gryphon whispers and runs his hands down my naked back until they come to rest on my arse. I hope Sophie didn't see that. "Not that I'm complaining."

"I'll get you something to wear," Sophie announces and runs off. I almost forgot how intense she can be.

Gryphon presses one last kiss on my lips, then steps back but still keeps an arm around my waist. "Let's go inside. It's cold out here."

I'd love to reply with a line about him making me hot, but he's right, and besides, we're kind of exposed out here. The only other house nearby, the inn, is a ten-minute walk away, but you never know who might pass by. Not that I'd be embarrassed of my nakedness, no, but it would raise undesired attention.

He pulls me inside the cottage. The door is so low that even I have to bow my head. It's cosy inside, with an open fireplace giving both light and warmth. The cottage is one big room that includes a kitchen area to our left and old-fashioned sofas and armchairs to our right. Raised platforms on either side just below the roof, accessed by ladders, hide the sleeping quarters. There's only one door that I hope leads to a bathroom with a shower. This place looks kind of rustic so I hope there's hot, running water.

Sophie waves down from one of the balconies. "I found a nightie for you!"

She waves a white, frilly thing that I am most definitely not going to wear.

Gryphon chuckles. "She's quite a force of nature. It's clear that the two of you are related, even if you didn't look alike. We need to talk about her eye, but that's for later. Let's get you warmed up. Want me to help you shower?"

"I don't need-" I begin, but then think better of it. "Yes, I think I'm feeling a little weak. I'll need help. I absolutely can't shower on my own."

"I'd join you, but the bathroom is a little small," Lennox calls from one of the sofas. "But I'll make us some food while you're...cleaning yourself."

His words are one big innuendo. There's no jealousy though. He wants us to do this, and I don't feel any animosity from Ryker either. They're fine with sharing me. Not that I'd give them a choice; they're all mine, but it's nice that we don't have to argue.

Gryphon leads me to the bathroom and locks the door behind us - I assume for Sophie's sake. Lennox was right, it is tiny, just enough space for a shower, a narrow washing basin and a toilet that's seen better days. Let's hope those cracks in the porcelain don't mean that it'll collapse as soon as I take a seat on it.

As soon as Gryphon rips off his clothes, all thoughts of our surroundings disappear. All I have eyes for is him. Has he always been this gorgeous? His scars only highlight his beautiful grass-green eyes and strong jaw. And that hair...I run my hands through it and tousle his mane. His beard has grown long while we were apart. I like it, it makes him look a little more rogue.

"Lily has been telling me to shave it off," he mutters. "I told her I'd only do it once we'd found you. Now it's your decision."

"How romantic," I tease. "You're offering me your beard? Will there be classical music in the background as you shave it off?"

"Of course. And rose petals on the floor. But do you really want me to shave it off? I think it makes me look more masculine."

I can't help but snort. "You always look masculine, beard or no beard." I tousle my fingers in his coarse beard hair. It's not as spiky as it used to be when his beard was a lot shorter. I kind of like it. If he lets it grow even more, it might become soft. That will feel nice while kissing...

"Keep it, but if you get mites or bedbugs in it, I'll shave it off myself."

He rolls his eyes. "I'm not intending to make it a home for critters. Unless you're one of them." He winks in the most cheesy way possible. I think it's time to end this conversation and focus on the more important things.

"Didn't you want to help me shower? I'm feeling a little too tired to do it on my own."

I give him an innocent smile and flutter my eyelashes.

"Are you having a stroke?" he asks with a frown.

"Huh?"

"Your eyelids are twitching weirdly."

I groan. "That was supposed to look endearing. Maybe alluring."

Gryphon clears his throat. "Maybe stick to just smiling next time. You're not really the fluttering type."

I punch him in the stomach - lightly. More of a nudge. He takes the hint and pulls me close until our naked bodies mould into each other.

I lean up to kiss him, the shower all but forgotten. It's him I want. More than hot water. More than food. More than anything. I need him. He's mine and I want to show him. Despite everything that's happened, it feels like no time at all has passed when he slides into me. It's like he's coming home.

* * * * * *

IT TAKES TWO SHOWERS BEFORE WE EMERGE FROM THE bathroom. One to get clean, and the second after Gryphon seduced me into another round of sex. Not that I'm complaining. I'm exhausted but in a good, pleasant way.

The hot water has softened my muscles and I'm all relaxed now, for the first time in months.

"That took a long time," Sophie complains. "The food went cold."

She's playing some kind of board game with Lennox, while Ryker is curled up on the sofa with a book. My heart aches a little at the sight. It's so...family. Mundane. Beautiful.

Yet I stand there, not quite sure what to do. Shall I join them? Will that destroy the illusion of peace? Maybe it's better if I stay apart. I don't want this moment to end.

Gryphon gently pushes me forward, towards the closest sofa. "Sit down, I'll get you some food."

I'm glad he's told me what to do. I let him steer me to the sofa and sit down with a soft sigh. I'm suddenly really tired. I need to sleep as soon as I've eaten something. I truly want to make plans for what to do next, but the presence of the guys gives me the confidence to put that off until tomorrow. If something bad happens, they'll be here to help me. It's strange how I've come to trust them. Now even more than before the kidnapping. I guess I've realised how much they mean to me, how much I value them. Before, I kept trying to persuade myself that I didn't need them, that I could be happy on my own if I wanted to. Our long separation has shown me how important they are. How much I love them.

Look at me, all sappy and emotional. Talking about love. Old-Kat would puke up a hairball at seeing me like this, but I think I've changed for the better.

Gryphon hands me a plate of sausages, mash and cabbage. I look up at him in surprise. That's some surprisingly good food. I was expecting canned beans and bread.

"I got some supplies at the local market when I picked

up Ryker in Lakeside," he explains. "That's the closest village. Technically, both this cottage and the inn by the bridge are part of it, although it's a brisk half-hour walk from here. Far enough to have privacy but close enough to get some decent food."

I tuck in and forget the world around me. These sausages are my new best friends. I devour them in record time. Two new ones appear on my plate. I don't look up to thank whoever got them for me; I'm way too busy eating.

"I can make some more," Lennox offers. "We need to get some meat on your bones again. You look starved."

"Way to compliment a lady," Gryphon snickers. "Have you no manners at all?"

"Just telling the truth. I don't want to fear that I might break her when she's in my arms."

"You're not going to break me," I protest, but only half the words are audible thanks to me still chewing on a particularly large piece of sausage.

"My mother said Kat should be kept hungry," Sophie mutters without looking up from the game. "The servants made sure not to give her too much."

An uncomfortable silence falls. I don't know how much Sophie has told them about how she was brought up, but judging from their stunned looks, she's not spoken about what her so-called parents did to me.

"Did she say why?" Gryphon asks, sounding as if someone's strangling him.

"She said Kat would get angry if she got too much food, and that would make the process slower."

Lennox stops playing and stares at her. "What process?"

"They wanted to make her my friend, but she was too naughty. My father said that she'd try to hurt me if they let me play with her, so they had to change her. They wanted to stop her from being naughty."

Okay, that makes no sense whatsoever.

"I would never have hurt you, Sophie, I hope you know that," I tell her while looking right into her remaining eye. The other one is hidden behind a red scarf that she's wrapped around her head. "You're my sister and there's no way I could have harmed you. Or would harm you now."

"But they said-"

"Not everything your parents said is true," I interrupt her. "They didn't like your name. They didn't want you to have a favourite colour. And you instinctively knew that wasn't right. Listen to your heart, Sophie. You know that it wasn't right of them to let me starve. You know it wasn't because I was naughty."

She looks at me for almost a minute without speaking, then nods.

"I like having a sister," she says quietly. "And you didn't like the lab either. We're the same. I know I said you weren't my sister, but I lied. I really like you."

"The lab?" Ryker asks sharply. "What did they do to you, Kat?"

"The lab?" I repeat. "I was in no lab. I was kept in a cell the entire time and was only transferred into a different room in the last few days before we escaped."

Sophie shakes her head. "You were in the lab many times. I watched you. Sometimes, I had to be there too so they could compare us. You were always sleeping, though. You're quite the sleepy head."

Fuck. I knew they'd sometimes knocked me out with that gas, but I had no recollection of ever being taken out of my cell. There had never been any signs that I'd been moved. Whatever they'd done to me had left no traces.

I shake my head to get rid of all the images popping

into my mind. What they may have done. So many possibilities. All of them scary.

Gryphon puts his hands on my shoulders and squeezes them softly. "We'll figure it out, Kat. Don't freak out."

"I don't freak out," I protest, but my voice shivers close to the hysteria spectrum. This isn't the first time I've been treated like a lab rat. And it's also not the first time that I can't remember it. Grandma Doctor, Mystery Man, they'd all experimented on me without me having any recollection of it. It makes me feel more vulnerable than I'd like. I think I'd rather have memories of whatever they did to me than have it left to speculation.

"What did they do to you both?" Ryker asks Sophie.

You could hear a grain of sand hit the floor.

To my surprise, Sophie looks at me with excitement. "I'm going to be an aunt."

"What the fuck," Ryker curses, vocalising exactly what I'm thinking.

Sophie can't mean what I think she means...right?

"What are you saying?" Lennox demands forcefully. I'd tell him off for speaking to my sister in that way, but I can't focus on anything but the echo of her words still ringing in my head. *I'm going to be an aunt.*

"You're going to have a baby," she says to me as if that's the most natural thing in the world. "That means I'm going to be an aunt."

All three guys look at me, just as confused as I am.

"I'm not sure how much you know about how babies are made, Sophie, but I can't be pregnant. There's no way."

As far as I know, shifter pregnancies are pretty similar to human ones, which would mean that since I've been away from the guys for several months, I should show signs by now. I look down at my belly. No bump. Definitely not. And I can't hear a heartbeat either. I have no idea when a foetus's heart first starts beating, but there's nothing to be heard.

Besides, I don't know if I even can get pregnant. I'm a clone; I wasn't born like normal people. I might be compatible with Ryker since he's a cat shifter too, but he's a house cat while I'm a panther. I doubt I'd be able to have a child with Lennox. I've heard rumours of shifters having kids with humans, but is Gryphon human enough for that?

I've never really thought about having children. I'm not the maternal type, not in the slightest. I'd probably teach my child to kill before they can even walk. No, Sophie is not going to be an aunt, I can guarantee that.

"Yes, you are pregnant," she insists. "My mother showed me on the screen. It didn't look like a baby yet but she said that's going to change before it's born. Are you excited?"

I want to shake her and force her to tell me what the hell is going on, but at the same time, I'm sad at her innocent excitement.

I feel sick. And it's not morning sickness. I can't be pregnant. No fucking way.

"Sophie, did your parents say who the father is?" Lennox asks gentler her than I could.

She nods, still smiling. I can't look at her.

"It's my father," Sophie says with more innocence than I can handle. "But that's okay, because I'm adopted, so I won't really be the babies' sister. I'll be their aunt because I'm Sophie's sister. My mother explained it all. We were all going to live together. Kat as my friend and the babies-"

I run to the bathroom and just about manage to reach the toilet before I throw up. I heave and heave, almost grateful for the acid burn in my throat. It distracts me from what I just heard.

It can't be. She's lying. Or they fed her wrong

information. It can't be true. I'm not pregnant. And I'm definitely not carrying that murderous siren's child. I never even saw him while I was held prisoner. His wife was the only one who visited me.

No. I refuse this to be true.

Ryker's scent announces him moments before he wraps his arms around me. With one hand, he holds my hair back while I throw up again, while he soothingly rubs my belly with the other. I hiss at the touch and he immediately realises his mistake. He moves his arm up until he's just below my boobs. Far away from uterus territory.

Gryphon joins us in the bathroom, making it seem even smaller.

"Are you alright?" he asks in his doctor voice. "I'm going to get you a pregnancy test as soon as the shops open in the morning."

Instead of an answer, I throw up again. My knees are wobbly with exhaustion and shock. I'm glad Ryker is holding me or I might end up on the floor. Although that would fit the way I feel. Absolutely rotten.

What happened to me in that house? Did Delaney rape me while I was unconscious? Did he somehow artificially inseminate me? The thought makes me sick again.

I zone out of reality and only dimly feel the guys cleaning me up and putting me to bed. I can't even talk. It's too much. I don't think I've ever felt worse than right now. Being imprisoned in a tiny cell, being tortured, starved, was nothing compared to this.

I'm going to be an aunt.

Sophie's voice echoes through my mind, again and again until I want to scream to drown her out.

The guys curl up around me, hold me, whisper reassurances, but while it takes the edge off the pain a little, it's not enough.

I'm going to be an aunt.

Fuck you, Sophie. You're not going to be an aunt. No way. Even if I have to cut that abomination out of me myself.

❊ ❊ ❊ ❊ ❊ ❊

THE NIGHT IS OVER FAR TOO SOON. I DOUBT I SLEPT, EVEN though I drifted off a couple of times. I'm even more exhausted than I was before I lay down. My stomach cramps with hunger; what a waste for those sausages to end up in the toilet.

Gryphon and Lennox leave the bed in the early morning, but Ryker stays with me, holding me from behind. I breathe in his feline scent. It's soothing, reminding me of home.

"How's Pumpkin?" I ask in the hope this might take my mind off things.

"Very well. He's grown a lot in the last few months, you'll be surprised when you see him. He misses you, of course, but he's also been very busy building up his own little gang of young street cats. It's adorable, although he'd kill me for saying so. I'm proud, though. He's a born leader."

"Just like his dad."

"His dad only became a leader because he had to," Ryker mutters with an air of regret. "I would have preferred to stay in the shadows, but I couldn't sit back when there were ways I could help. I'd never planned to create an entire community for cats, but it happened and I'm proud of it. I just don't like always having to be in charge."

"You could train Pumpkin to be your assistant. It sounds like he's doing that himself already."

Ryker sighs. "I tried to keep him away from the responsibility because I wanted him to have a long, happy childhood, but it seems you're right, he's decided to venture on that path by himself. I wonder sometimes if he feels he has to prove something to me because we don't know if he'll ever be able to shift. I keep telling him that I love him no matter what, but I think he's worried he might stay a cat forever despite his heritage."

"It must be hard for him. If you want, I can have a chat with him when we're back. Sometimes it's good to hear the truth from someone other than your parents."

He nods, rubbing his cheek against the back of my head. "I'd appreciate it. He adores you. Come to think of it, I owe him for introducing us. Without him, we'd never have met."

"He deserves a medal. And a lifetime supply of catnip."

"Don't you dare turn my son into an addict," he warns with a laugh. "It's bad enough watching you get stoned on that stuff."

"I don't get stoned. I relax and enjoy it like a true connoisseur."

"Of course you do. I'll remind you of that the next time you're chasing a ball of string while rubbing your arse against the kitchen cupboards."

"I do not-" I sigh. "I don't suppose you brought some catnip with you? I could do with some of that now."

"I'm afraid not. But I can make you some breakfast. I've been learning to cook while you were away. Bethany says my fried eggs are the best she's ever had."

"I guess you'll have to prove that now. With bacon?"

"And onions. If Gryphon bought some. I doubt he got any parsley but you'll get the luxury version when we're back in Attenburgh, I promise."

My stomach growls in appreciation. I don't quite want

to get up yet, though. For a moment, I was able to forget what happened. I don't want it all to come crashing back.

"Lennox has gone to get a pregnancy test," Ryker says as if he read my mind. "And Gryphon was planning to talk to Sophie again to find out what else she knows. The two of them have a good bond and she trusts him. We thought it's better if he does that rather than you. Less stress for both you and Sophie."

While I agree, I can't help but feel left out. They decided this without me. Granted, I was completely out of it last night and not capable of making decisions, but it still hurts.

"Want to help me make breakfast or shall I serve you breakfast in bed?"

A polite Kat would say she'd help...but that's not me.

"Breakfast in bed sounds wonderful."

He presses a kiss on the nape of my neck. "Then so be it. I'll be back soon. Shout if you need anything."

He makes it sound like I'm an invalid who needs help with everything. Or maybe like I'm a Queen to be waited on. Yes, let's go with that one. It's less depressing.

With him gone, I'm left to my own thoughts once again. I'm both hopeful and anxious about that pregnancy test. Hopefully, it'll prove that Sophie's pretend-parents told her lies. They manipulated her in so many ways that this might be just one of their methods to keep her under their control. I wonder why she never mentioned anything while we were running though.

I need to think of something else. Distract myself. Until now, I've ignored the whispers coming from the second balcony at the other end of the room. Sophie is talking to Gryphon, just like Ryker said.

I focus on them until their hushed voices become audible. I shouldn't snoop, but they both know that I'm very capable of listening to their conversation. Four out of the five of us are shifters with superior hearing. If they wanted me not to hear, they would have left the house.

"Do you know when your father did this to Kat?" Gryphon asks Sophie.

"I'm not quite sure. Maybe two weeks ago? Or three? That's why they gave her a new room, to make her more comfortable for the babies."

I suck in a sharp breath. Did she just say *babies*? Plural? Fuck me. I'm going to have a litter. Like a cat. No freaking way. I refuse to.

"You said they showed you on a screen. Did you see how many babies she's carrying?" Gryphon's voice is strained. I admire him for keeping this calm while talking to her.

"Four. It was five but one disappeared from the scanner. My father was quite angry about that."

I think I'm about to faint. Four babies. Inside of me. It can't be right. I has to be one big joke.

The door opens and Lennox enters the cottage, waving a bag.

"Kat, come down, I've got the test."

I swallow hard. It's time to find out the truth.

CHAPTER EIGHTEEN

I have to stop the guys from following me into the bathroom to watch me pee on that plastic stick. It's hard enough already to get myself to pee even though I don't have to and even though all my insides are clenched with fear. I'm not sure I've ever been this scared in all my life.

When I step out of the bathroom, they all crowd around me, including Sophie. She's almost jumping with excitement, while the rest of us are gloomy and worried. If she mentions how she's looking forward to being an aunt one more time, I'm going to disinherit her.

I shake the stick as instructed, waiting for it to change colour. Green for pregnant, red for not. Please turn red. Please.

The edges of the stick take on a pale green sheen and I let it drop to the floor. The universe hates me.

Ryker takes me in his arms while Gryphon bends down to pick up the test. He stares at it, shaking it again as if to force it to change colour. But it stays green.

"Fuck," Lennox exhales. "You're going to have puppies."

"Kittens," Ryker corrects.

Gryphon frowns at them. "Babies."

"I don't care what you call them," I hiss, close to shouting hysterically. "There are things growing inside of me. Get them out!"

Ryker rubs my back in an effort to soothe me, but there's no calming me down. I grasp my stomach, my claws ready to shoot out and tear myself open. I can't take this. Someone put babies into me and there's nothing I can do about it. No, not someone. Delaney. I'm going to kill him. Slow and painfully. Let him suffocate on his dick while ripping him apart, limb by limb. I can't wait to see him dead.

"Let's kill him," I snarl. "Kill that bastard."

"Kat, calm down," Ryker whispers with a purr. "Sit. Breathe. This isn't the time to do anything rash. We need to figure out what exactly happened to you."

Gryphon nods. "Just because the pregnancy test was positive doesn't mean you're actually going to have babies. It could be a false positive. You've been through a lot and that can get your hormones disrupted. Once we're back in Attenburgh, we can do an ultrasound and see what's happening, alright?"

"No," I hiss. "I need to know now. How would you feel knowing that parasites are growing within you? You're the doctor. Operate, get them out of me."

He shakes his head. "I can't just cut you open. We need more information before we can make any such decision."

Lennox takes my hand and gently guides me to the closest sofa. He sits down and pulls me into his lap. I let him do it. I don't have the strength to fight back.

"We're here with you," he says with emphasis. "We'll be

with you every step of the way, no matter what happens. If you're really having puppies...babies, then so be it. We'll raise them as our own. Right, guys?"

Ryker and Gryphon grunt in agreement.

"Even if that bastard siren is the father, that still means that half of their genes are given by you. Those children will be amazing because you are amazing. And we'll make sure they have the best childhood they could possibly imagine. There's four of us, so even if you have a litter of four, we can handle one each."

I can't get my head around that number. Four babies. That's four more than I ever wanted. As nice as he makes it sound, having a family with loving fathers, it's not what I want. It wasn't my decision and that's what matters.

"I'm so looking forward to-" Sophie says cheerily.

"Get her out of here!" I shout, unable to even look at her.

Gryphon gently leads her out of the cottage, leaving me with Lennox and Ryker. Lennox holds me tight while Ryker massages my shoulders. I sense their helplessness with every touch. They don't know what to do any more than I do. We've been thrown into an impossible situation and there doesn't seem to be a way out of it.

I'm still tempted to simply claw my belly open and rip out my uterus. My healing powers should be strong enough to deal with that by now. And if I fall unconscious, even better. I don't want to be able to think. I just want to sleep and forget about it all. Go back to life before I was self-kidnapped.

How is it that you never know how good your life is until it's taken away from you? I'd love to tell the Kat of the past to enjoy her time with the guys, with M.E.O.W., because it won't last forever. Now, it's too late. My old life has been torn away from me and there's no way I'll ever get it back. We might return to a semblance of normality, but the scars of the past will always be there. And four of those scars might turn out to be living, breathing, crying babies. Could I even love them? I highly doubt it. They're not mine, not really. I had no part in it besides lending my eggs and uterus. I'm basically a surrogate. And genes don't really matter. Aunt Rose is the best example of that. She took in my younger siblings and loves them as much as her own daughter, even though she's not related to them.

"Kat, stop."

Lennox pulls my hands off my belly and clasps them tight. Bloodstains show on my shirt. I hadn't even realised that I'd partially shifted, turning my fingernails into sharp claws. I don't feel the pain. I'm numb, mentally and physically. I don't think I could cry, even if I was the kind of person who cried when she got emotional.

Ryker squeezes my shoulders a little harder as if to pull me from my stupor.

"What can we do to make it better?" he asks gently. "How can we help?"

"Kill them," I scoff. "Kill those parasites. And then help me kill Delaney and his fucking wife."

"We'll definitely kill them, soon," he says, his voice hard. "There's no doubt about that. As soon as we've regrouped with the others, we can start making plans. Right now, it would be too much of a risk. You're in no state to fight - no, don't protest, you know I'm right. You're half-starved and you still need to process everything that happened. We can't be impulsive about this. He's too powerful to take on while we're not at full strength."

"I agree with Ryker." Lennox presses a kiss on my shoulder. I don't even care. They could fuck me and I wouldn't feel anything.

They keep talking, trying to calm me down, trying to

find reasons why this isn't the worst situation ever, but I barely get myself to listen. Maybe I should shift. Let my cat take control again. She was right; she's stronger than me.

After a while, Gryphon joins us. "Sophie is looking after the horses. She's really good with them. I've told her we're going to get her a pony when we're back home."

He waits for a reaction from me, but when nothing comes, he sighs and takes a seat next to Lennox, on whose lap I'm still perched.

"I don't have any way to examine you. The nearest hospital is probably in the Capital, but that's way too dangerous. Of course, going back to Attenburgh is dangerous too because Lord Delaney knows where we live, but at least there we'll have the protection of Lady Lara as well as having the other M.E.O.W. members around. Plus Ryker's cats who can help keep watch. So I think we should get back there as soon as possible. Lady Lara can arrange for me to examine you at the hospital and use their equipment, without anyone asking questions. She might even know some experts who can be bribed not to talk."

"What use will examining me do?" I ask tonelessly. "Just cut it out. Get rid of it. Job done."

"Kat," Lennox whispers and pulls me even closer. "You can't think like that. Not yet. Once we're back in Attenburgh and know what exactly that fucker did to you, we can talk about it. If it only happened three weeks ago at most, there's lots of time before it's too late. You never know, they might be clones again. Little baby Kats. That would be kind of cute."

"Not as cute as baby Gryphons," the siren quips.

I can't share his humour. I know he's trying to make light of the situation, cheer me up, but it's no use. I won't be able to forget how hopeless it all is.

"How long will it take us to get to Attenburgh?" I ask. My voice barely sounds like my own.

"With the horses, if we ride all day with only short breaks at night, ten days," Gryphon replies. "But more likely two weeks. It's autumn and we can't expect the weather to be good every day. Plus we have Sophie; she might need more rests than we do. We can't forget she's still a child. She may not always behave like it, but she's young and can't always keep up with us."

Two weeks. My stomach turns.

"How long until a foetus develops a heartbeat?"

He clears his throat, clearly uncomfortable. "Usually at nine to ten weeks, but that's for humans. Sirens have a shorter pregnancy than humans, and I have no idea about shifters."

"Shorter than humans, too," Lennox says. "For wolf shifters, it's about six months. Ryker, do you know how long your cat girlfriend was pregnant for? I know she was a pure cat but since you're a shifter, it might help to know."

"Pumpkin came to me about three months after I'd slept with her. He was only a few days old so it must have been about that long. Usually, cat pregnancies only last two months or so, which means me being a shifter must have made it longer."

Six months. Three months. I shudder at the thought. I don't know any cat shifters besides Ryker who I could ask. And even if I did, I have no idea how long a siren-shifter pregnancy would last. If I indeed carry Lord Delaney's child. *Children.* A cold shiver runs down my back. Knowing the kind of stuff he did to Sophie, I'm not even sure it's really his genetic material. It might be some kind of experiment yet again. What would be the worst-case scenario? Those grunts? Something monstrous that would make my babies look like aliens? Or maybe he succeeded in creating the easy-to-control, powerful shifters he seems to want. A child that follows every command. Like the Pack tried with Little Kat and Caitlin. That always seems to be their goal. Turning us into slaves; soldiers. They can't just let us live in peace. No, they envy us for our strength and want to control us. I wonder if that's an intrinsic siren thing. I suppose it's part of their nature to control and manipulate other beings. Their experiments and cloning just takes that one step further.

Luckily, Gryphon is different from the rest of his family, as is Auntie Rose and her daughter. Proof that genetics aren't everything.

"We'll figure it out," Gryphon says softly. "Once I get access to an ultrasound machine, we'll see how developed they already are and that can give us a hint to how long the pregnancy will last."

"I don't want it to last. I want it to end, right now."

Suddenly, a new sound reaches my ears and I freeze. Lennox and Ryker must have heard the same thing for they stare at me in shock.

I look down at my belly in disbelief.

It's a heartbeat that wasn't there a moment ago.

CHAPTER NINETEEN

I'm going crazy. I really am. Going feral was nothing compared to this. I hold my head in my hands, unable to deal with this new development.

There's a heart beating inside my belly. No, inside my uterus. It's no longer just a hypothetical parasite growing in there. It's a baby.

Only one heartbeat for now, thank the Catnip Gods. I think I'd faint if there were more than one.

"Three instead of nine weeks," Gryphon mutters to himself. "That could mean the pregnancy will be over in three months instead of nine. We need to get to Attenburgh as soon as possible."

I ignore his words. I can't even consider that possibility.

"Can I?" Ryker asks and points at my stomach. I think he wants to listen closer.

"No," I growl. "Don't touch me."

He backs off but keeps his hands on my shoulders. I'm grateful; his gentle massage helps ground me a little. As does Lennox's embrace. Gryphon is the only one not touching me. He jumped up when the guys told him they could hear a heartbeat and has now returned with a stethoscope.

"Can I?" he repeats Ryker's question.

Grudgingly, I let him. It's different with him; he does it as a medical professional rather than out of pure curiosity like Ryker.

He pulls up my shirt and gently moves the stethoscope until he finds the perfect position.

"Your hearing really is amazing," he whispers. "I can barely hear it. If I didn't know it was there, I may have not even picked up on it. It's only one, right?"

I nod. "Thank goodness. Imagine if-"

A second heartbeat echoes the first, a little faster.

Fuck.

"A second heartbeat has just appeared," Ryker tells Gryphon.

The siren repositions the stethoscope, but he seems unable to find the second sound. It is a little fainter than the first, but I'm sure it'll catch up soon. If it continues like this, I should hear four different heartbeats within the next few minutes. I think my mind is about to burst. I don't know what to think. It's like my body no longer belongs to me. I feel detached from it, like I'm looking at it from a distance. It's almost calming to have that separation. I can think more clearly, analysing what's going on.

"Third," Lennox says at the same time as I pick up on the sound.

I want to faint. Can I make myself faint somehow? I remember the time I made Ryker sit on my throat until I passed out. He still makes fun of that. How a house cat suffocated a panther several times his size. I doubt he'll do me the same favour right now, though. The guys want me to face reality, even though I'm not ready to do so.

Two minutes of waiting later, the fourth heartbeat pops

into existence. This one is slower than the other three, but a little louder, even compared to the first.

Four fricking babies. Bloody hell. A whole litter of kittens. Except that they may or may not be kittens.

Sophie said the fifth foetus didn't make it, but all of us wait a bit more nonetheless. To my relief, no further heartbeat is added. It's already four too many. They echo through the room, louder than drums. I can barely think with them filling my ears.

"Now I can hear them too," Gryphon whispers, an expression of awe on his face. "Four heartbeats. This is adorable."

Not what I'd call it. Horrifying, more like. It's freaking me out. I want to scream and rip off my clothes and throw myself on the floor in a childlike tantrum. Yet none of that even comes close to expressing how I feel.

"You look like you're about to pass out." Gryphon looks at me with concern. "Are you in pain?"

I laugh. Understatement of the century. I'm in agony, mentally. I'm being torn apart.

He takes my wrist to take my pulse and again, I laugh. Suddenly, it all seems comical.

I'm having babies growing inside of me. Real babies. The universe is having a laugh. I must be the least maternal person out there, yet I'm the one about to be a mother. I'm going to have to press four babies out of my vagina. It'll never be the same again. Flabby and loose. The guys will have lots of room inside of me. I snicker.

"What?" Lennox asks.

"Just thinking of my vagina."

I didn't quite intend to actually say that out loud. Oops.

"You've got a lovely vagina," Gryphon says with a grin. "She's beautiful."

Heat draws over my cheeks. Not the conversation I was planning to have.

"Yes, lovely vagina," Ryker adds. "Why are we talking about your vagina though?"

"Because these parasites are going to destroy it. Tear me apart. Imagine what I'll look like after popping out four abominations at once."

"They'll come out one after the other," Gryphon explains as if that wasn't clear. "And the female body is made to do that. Women have been giving birth for hundreds of thousands of years. You're not the first and you won't be the last."

I glare at him. "Not the point."

"We can take some pictures of it," Lennox suggests. "Put them on the wall as a reminder of how your vagina used to look like."

I elbow him in the ribs and he yelps. "Again, not the point."

A knock on the door signals Sophie returning. "Can I come in now?"

I sigh. At least this random talk about my inner sanctum has dispelled some of the gravity. I still don't want these babies, but at least I'm no longer frozen by fear and panic.

Gryphon exchanges a look with me and I give him a nod. I know it's not my sister's fault. She's only the messenger, but now I know why kings often kill those.

"Come in," Gryphon shouts and Sophie immediately strolls into the room. "How are the horses?"

"Knickerbocker almost ate my hand," she tells us with a wide grin. "He had three apples and still wanted more. Lucy licked my face and I brushed Kidril. He let me touch him this time." She seems proud of that. "I think he might become my friend if I brush him every day."

"You can do that," Gryphon says with a smile that reminds me of a proud father looking at his daughter. "You can even ride him if you want. With one of us; we don't have a horse for everyone. We're leaving soon, so better pack your bags."

She nods and climbs up to one of the balconies. She no longer seems to have any hesitation about leaving her home and venturing into an unknown city with people she only met days ago.

I don't have any belongings to pack, but Ryker and Gryphon get up to sort out their stuff. Lennox keeps me on his lap, nuzzling my neck. I both want to lean into his embrace and jump up and run. My mind is a little calmer after all that pussy talk, but I'm still on edge. One tiny push and I'll be back in turmoil.

"I can't wait to be back home." Lennox runs a hand through my hair. "It'll all be back to normal."

"It'll never be normal again. Everything has changed. Now that we know what Delaney did to me, he won't ever let me run around free. He'll come for me and his offspring. I doubt he cares if I'm dead or alive as long as I serve as an incubator and egg donor for him. He might leave me alone until I've given birth, but then he'll come, I guarantee you."

"Then we'll be ready to fight."

"I don't just want to defend," I snap more harshly than I intended. "I want to bring the battle to him. Wipe him and his sirens out once and forever. Until he's gone, I won't be able to go back to how it used to be."

He licks my shoulder. Yes, he didn't kiss me, he licked me. Silly dog.

"Then so be it. We'll gather our allies and fight. But first, let us get back home. Lily was incredibly jealous that she wasn't the first one to meet you. It took quite a bit of persuading on Gryphon's part to make her stay in Attenburgh and coordinate everything from there. Same with Caitlin. We almost had to chain her up. She wanted to search for you too, but we managed to get her to understand that it wasn't safe for her. Not just because we don't know if she could go back to her mind-controlled state, but also because she'll be valuable to anyone finding out who and what she is. Just like all of you."

I nod, glad he and the guys talked sense into Lily and Caitlin. I would have said the same. "Have you heard from Little Kat and the twins? Are they okay?"

"Yes, they're fine. We didn't tell them that you were missing. Auntie Rose knows, but she agreed to keep it quiet for now. We didn't want to scare the girls. I bet the twins would have immediately come to Attenburgh to help and of course that would have caused even more chaos."

I can imagine them running around town, asking every single person they pass about me. With their knives at their throats. Yeah, that would have not gone down well. Besides, I don't want them to get messed up in my life. They're children and they deserve to have a decent childhood and education.

"We should get ready," Lennox sighs.

"I don't have anything to pack."

He chuckles. "Oh, you do. Gryphon got you some clothes from the market and we all have one of your knives for you. When we started our search, we each took one with the aim of being the first to give you back your weapons. Now, all three of us can do it at the same time."

My heart clenches with love and pain. It's such a sweet gesture. They brought me my favourite daggers. Other women might be happy with flowers. I get emotional over blades.

"Thank you. I better get changed then."

"If Sophie wasn't in the room, I'd ask you to change in front of me," he whispers and licks my neck again. "But I'll be sure to watch you undress tonight. I promise."

I roll my eyes. Men.

Gryphon bought me two outfits, both of them simple and comfortable. They're not the black leather I prefer, but that would stand out too much. I change into a moss green tunic and thick brown trousers perfect for sitting on a saddle all day. He even thought of a sheath for my knives. The way to a girl's heart is through a pretty sheath.

By the time we're all ready to leave, the sun has risen and shines into the cosy cottage. I'm almost sorry to leave this place. Maybe we should come here again, one day in the far future, and have a holiday. Just me and the guys. We've earned ourselves a break.

Not yet, though. First, we've got a long journey ahead of us, and then, a battle for survival. Talk about high stakes.

Since there are only three horses, Sophie rides with Gryphon and I end up sitting in front of Ryker. I wish I had my own horse, but it makes sense for the two smallest to share with the guys. Lennox smirks happily at having a horse for himself.

"Can I hold the reins?" Sophie asks excitedly and Gryphon hands them to her with an indulgent smile. The two of them are rather cute together. My little sister's eyes are hidden beneath a large-rimmed straw hat and I know she has some sunglasses in her pocket should it get too windy for the hat. Gryphon hasn't had the chance yet to talk to me about her eye. Not that we can do anything about it while we're on the road.

Yet another reason to get home as quickly as possible.

I look around our small group and nod to myself. Time to ride.

CHAPTER TWENTY

The first three days pass quickly. We ride all day with only a short break for lunch and to let the horses drink. We spend the nights in abandoned buildings that we come across; a small shed, a cottage not dissimilar to the one we started out from, and a stable with a leaky roof. Even three hours away from that one, I can still smell the rotten hay.

Sophie is sleeping in Gryphon's arms, exhausted from the hard pace we're setting. She hasn't complained though. She's refused to ride with anyone but Gryphon. I think he's flattered by her clinginess. Her attitude towards me has grown a little colder though. I assume she's not forgiven me yet for shouting at her to get out of the room. I've not tried explaining why I did that. She wouldn't understand. She's mentioned being an auntie several more times, but I just tune her out whenever that happens. It's hard enough to constantly hear four quiet heartbeats within me. I no longer get freaked out by them; they've become part of me in a creepy, uncomfortable way.

Parasites. I can't think of them as babies, kittens, pups,

whatever. They're unwanted parasites. Gross and slimy. Feeding off me. I've already noticed that I'm hungrier than usual. I never stay sated for long. The guys have started carrying snacks around so that they can feed me whenever I get cranky. At least I don't have any morning sickness. Yet. If that happened, I'd go back to my plan of cutting them out of me.

"We're about to get close to Tahaven," Gryphon announces from the front of our little caravan. He's the one with the best geographical knowledge, courtesy of the private scholars his father paid for. Yet another reminder that he had a very different upbringing than the rest of us.

"It's a town that should give us any supplies we need, but if I remember correctly, quite a few siren families live here. It might be better to skirt the town and resupply in whatever village we pass next."

"What do we actually need?" Lennox asks from behind me. Today I'm riding with him on Knickerbocker, a large mare with a strong interest in brambles. She likes to stop at every bramble bush we come across. It's driving me crazy.

"We're going to run out of food tomorrow, with the way Kat's devouring our supplies." Gryphon grins at me. "And I'd like to stop by a pharmacy to get something for Sophie's eye. It's become itchy."

"I'm fine," Sophie protests, but even I have noticed that she keeps scratching her eye. We still call it the eye, even though technically it's gone. It's easier for all of us that way. We don't like reminding Sophie of it. On the outside, she seems to be coping well, but there are signs that she's upset and scared. She's my sister; I know the way I look when I'm hiding something and she's exactly the same.

"How about only one of us goes into Tahaven?" I suggest. "The rest of us can skirt the town and we'll meet on the other side."

Gryphon sighs. "I guess it should be me. Kat and Sophie definitely can't, Ryker's eyes make him stand out, and Lennox...yes, I'll do it."

"What's with me?" Lennox challenges.

The siren rolls his eyes. "You're rubbish at shopping. You can't tell one vegetable from another."

"If you're referring to the spinach versus kale incident, that wasn't my fault. Both are green leaves. They should have signs on them to tell which one's which."

I snicker. "What's that?"

"We had a leaf incident while you were gone," Gryphon explains. "Bethany needed kale for one of her weird potions and Lennox brought home an armful of spinach. She wasn't impressed."

"They looked the same," Lennox huffs. "How different can they be?"

I exchange a look with Gryphon and can't help but laugh. Even I know the difference and it's not like I'm a cook or botanist. "Yes, I think it's best if you go, Gryphon. Bring me some catnip?"

"No way. I need you sharp. I doubt Knickerbocker would appreciate you rolling all over her."

"I don't *roll*."

"You do," both Lennox and Gryphon retort. Ryker wisely stays quiet. I've caught him high on catnip and know that he behaves just as crazed as I do. We can't help it. We're cats. He told me once that some of the cats in his family don't react to catnip. I don't think that can be right. The thought makes me want to cuddle those cats in sympathy. To never know the joys of a large dose of catnip...poor babies.

"Two hours," I tell him to stop the Kat bashing. "If you're not back then, I'll send Lennox after you."

He nods and steers his horse closer to Ryker. "Sophie, jump over."

She grumbles complaints under her breath but does as he says. He's the only one who can order her around. Me, sometimes, and she mostly ignores the other guys. No idea what's so special about Gryphon in her eyes. Lennox and Ryker are just as kind to her as him and they're trying hard to make her trust them.

Ryker gently holds her and lets her take the reins. She's proven to be a great rider; better than me by miles. She'll definitely get a pony once we're back in Attenburgh. Or even a proper horse. I've watched her jump onto Kidril without any help. I think she uses her shifter strength to do so, even though she's not expressed any desire to shift since she's been with us.

I'm aching to shift, but I'm scared of what might happen. I can't afford to go feral again. I'll just have to suppress the urge and stay human. I managed for months in Lord Delaney's dungeon.

Gryphon gallops away to the town in the distance. The rest of us leave the road and continue cross-country, circling Tahaven over barren fields until we return to the road an hour later. A small stream passes nearby and we let the horses drink their fill. I'm hungry again. Ryker hands me a sandwich without me even needing to say something. That's true love. Knowing your mate is starving.

I devour the sandwich as well as the chocolate Lennox gives me with a wide grin. Both men watch me eat with fascination. Sophie couldn't care less. She's brushing the horses while they drink, ignoring us adults.

Lennox stretches and rolls his shoulders. "It smells like rain. Let's hope we find a nicer shelter than last night."

I don't sniff the air as I usually would. Using my senses automatically makes the four heartbeats louder, too loud for me to ignore. I'm shutting down my senses as much as possible, relying on the guys to warn me of any approaching threat. I hate doing it, but I'd go crazy if I constantly had to hear the parasites.

I copy Lennox, stretching and arching my back. I'm stiff from all the riding. I might go for a run tonight, as a human, not shifted. I need the exercise. The muscles I use while riding are very different from the ones I should be training to get back to my normal fitness.

"Kat?" Ryker stares at me. Not at my face. At my belly.

I look down. And look again. And run my hands over my stomach.

"What is it?" Lennox asks with concern and walks to Ryker's side so he can see me from the front.

Shivers run down my back. My legs start shaking. And the world suddenly seems a lot darker than before.

I have a bump. Small, but visible. And it wasn't there this morning. I washed myself in a pond by the stables and my stomach was just as flat as always then. Well, flatter than normal; I still need to regain both fat and muscles.

"This can't be happening," I whisper in shock. "It's too soon."

Ryker goes on his knees in front of me, ignoring the muddy ground. He stares at my belly as if he's seeing it for the first time. He's not the only one who feels that way.

A fucking bump. After three weeks of pregnancy. At most. This isn't happening.

I want to scream. And then shift and run and forget about everything. Would the parasites stay within me if I shifted? Maybe they wouldn't survive. I take a deep breath and ready myself to shift. I'll control my cat, somehow. And even if not... would it be so bad to let her take over again?

"Kat, no," Ryker warns. "Don't do it."

He grasps me by the hips and pulls me closer. I stagger forward until his face is pressed against my belly. My bump.

I want to stop him, but I suddenly don't have the energy.

He closes his eyes and listens intently. I don't know what he's doing. He can hear the heartbeats from where he was before, he doesn't need to crush his ears against my belly. Silly cat.

"They're different," he whispers without moving away.

"Huh?"

"Their heartbeats have slightly different rhythms. One of them has something almost like an echo. Two are identical. I think you may have kittens after all. Or at least two kittens. I can tell them apart from human heartbeats."

I stare at him. What the fuck is he saying? That I'm going to have four different babies? A mixed litter like a cat?

I need some catnip to deal with this. Right now.

"Let me listen."

Lennox kneels next to Ryker and puts his ear on my bump too. I look at my two guys, kneeling at my feet. I'm kind of tempted to ruffle their hair. Or tell them off like little boys. They look so cute when they're smaller than me.

"He's right," Lennox mutters. "They really are different. Do you think you'll have two kittens and two sirens?"

I push them away and step back, quickly smoothing my shirt to hide the bump. "I'm not going to have anything. Stop making them sound like actual babies. They're parasites that were put into me without my knowing. I'm not going to pretend everything's normal, even if you seem to be intent on doing so."

Lennox gets to his feet and gives me an apologetic puppy dog look. I cringe. It's hard to withstand those big eyes.

"We're not saying it's normal. Not at all. What they did to you is horrific and I'll kill them myself as soon as I'll get my paws on them. But I'm trying to separate that from the pups. It's not their fault how they were conceived. We don't even know what they are exactly. They could be more clones, exactly like you."

"No, they can't, actually," Ryker interrupts. "Two are kittens, probably cat shifters, but the other two have different heartbeats. I've never listened to a human foetus's heartbeat so I have no idea if this could be it. Maybe I should go into town and do some research."

"You want to ask random human females whether you can put your head on their bellies?" Lennox laughs. "I don't think that would go down well."

"I don't need to get that close to them, wolf," Ryker says testily. "Maybe you need to with your tiny dog ears, but I don't."

"But you've got yellow eyes that stand out."

This time, Ryker doesn't reply. It's not like he can do anything about his eyes. I've always found it strange that he doesn't look completely human when he's shifted. All other shifters I know have human eyes. Some may have a bit of a feral appearance, but they pass as human.

"Nobody is going anywhere," I sigh. "We'll wait until Gryphon gets here and then we'll ride on. I want to get to Attenburgh before these parasites are big enough to crawl out of me."

That thought gives me the creeps. Last night, I dreamed that they tore open my belly and climbed out of me, leaving me a bloody mess. They then proceeded to eat me, but luckily I woke up. I'd never been this grateful for Lennox's snoring.

Sophie has stayed quiet, tending to the horses, but now she turns around and looks at my bump. "Have you thought what you're going to call them?"

Both men freeze, probably expecting me to explode. And yes, I'm pretty close, but I just about manage to swallow my anger. It's not Sophie's fault. She's just a curious child who asks whatever's on her mind. She doesn't understand why I'm so upset. For her, it's all exciting and new. She wants to be an aunt. For someone who's grown up without siblings and raised by weird adoptive parents who experimented on her, that must be a dream come true.

My expression softens as I look at her.

"No, I've not thought about that. We don't know yet if they're going to be boys or girls. But maybe you can come up with some names? You can tell me your favourites when we get to Attenburgh."

Her eyes widen. "Really?"

I nod. "Really. But keep them a secret until we're home."

She grins happily and turns back to the horses, muttering under her breath. I think I heard "Little Sophie". I guess it's no worse than Little Kat, but I'll veto that name for sure.

"Well done," Ryker whispers. "Thank you."

"For what?"

He evades my eyes. He probably means for not shouting at Sophie or becoming a bubbling mess.

"I get it," I tell him. "I know."

CHAPTER TWENTY-ONE

Every day, the bump keeps growing. I can't look at my body anymore. It makes shivers run down my back. The guys are really supportive, feeding me snacks while we ride, but they can't dispel the fear still clouding my mind. I don't know what's growing inside me. Ryker may say that two of the heartbeats sound like kittens, but he could be wrong.

They're getting louder every day. I have to force myself to drone out the sound, which also means that the guys sometimes have to nudge me so that I realise they've been talking to me.

Today, I felt the first kick. We're still four days away from Attenburgh, although with the storm clouds quickly spreading across the sky, five days might be more likely. We already had to spend one full day holed up in an abandoned, leaky house a week ago when a storm tore through the land. Riding in almost no visibility and with rain turning the ground into sludge just wasn't feasible. I hated having to prolong our journey, but I'm still rational enough to accept reality. Most of the time.

At night, I still push out my claws and run the tips of them over my skin, so very tempted to cut open my belly. But now that I can hear and feel the beings growing inside me, it's no longer as easy. They're alive. And I don't know what to do.

"Kat?" Sophie calls from ahead of me. She's on Kidril with Gryphon as always. "Tell me how you met Gryphon. I don't believe his story."

Lennox snorts loud enough to equal my mare's regular snorting. "What have you been telling her, Gryph?"

"The truth," the siren protests. "How I sneaked into Kat's bedroom and clung to the ceiling like a spider, ready to drop down on her."

"Kat would never let you do that," Sophie insists. "She'd spot you right away. She's an assassin, you know?"

I suppress a laugh. Sophie has quite a high opinion of me. I don't want to squash that, but I also don't want to lie.

"It's mostly true," I admit. "He had climbed into my attic. I'd left the window open for Pumpkin, Ryker's son, who liked to visit me from time to time. But of course, I immediately knew that he was there and challenged him."

"Liar," Gryphon laughs. "You had no idea I was there. I could have slit your throat faster than you could have said 'catnip'."

I wish I had something less deadly than a knife to throw at him. I hate it when he tells the truth.

"Don't believe everything he says," I tell Sophie. "Rule number one: everybody lies."

"I never lie," he protests immediately. "I only twist the truth sometimes."

"That's lying," Sophie says sternly. "You shouldn't lie. My mother said lying makes you sick."

I both want to dispel that illusion and keep it for her to believe in.

"She lied," Lennox says before I can reply. "And because she didn't get sick, you know that's a lie."

Sophie turns around and frowns at him. "How do you know she didn't get sick? I'm not sure your logic is sound."

Ryker breaks into giggles and I'm having a hard time not doing the same. This girl is hilarious. It's hard to believe she's my sister.

"Shush," Gryphon suddenly hisses. "Look at that sign."

To our right, an old rusty sign has been overpainted with a few unsteady words.

KILL THE WOLVES.

"What do you think that means?" Lennox asks, worry lacing his tone. "Are they talking about actual wolves or werewolves?"

"I don't think there are any real wolves in this area," Gryphon says thoughtfully. "I can't be sure, but there are no forests anywhere nearby. Everything here is fields and farms; no place for a wolf pack to hide."

"I'll shift and see if I can find any traces." Lennox jumps off his horse in one elegant, fluid motion. It makes me want to lick him. We've not had any chance to be physical again since the cottage. We've always shared a room with Sophie. I can't wait to be back in our house in Attenburgh where we can choose from several bedrooms.

"Lennox, we don't have time," I tell him. "This doesn't concern us. We'll be home in a couple of days and will likely never come here again."

"It does concern us. If someone here is killing shifters, we need to do something about it."

One of the parasites uses that moment to kick me hard. I gasp and clutch my belly, regretting it immediately because it reminds me of my growing bump. My tunic stretches over my skin, even though it's supposed to be loose. The hem of my trousers is getting more and more uncomfortable. I may have to ask one of the guys if I can wear their clothes soon.

"Let him shift," Ryker says from behind me. "I agree, I want to know what's happening here."

"But what if we find out they're really hunting shifters?" I ask. "What do we do then? Stay here? Fight them? We can't. Look at me. I might be ready to pop within weeks. We need to get home."

"Just a few hours," Lennox begs. "Just to find out what's happening. If necessary, we can split up and I'll stay here. Or I'll contact my old contacts who might be able to help."

I sigh. If I wasn't pregnant, I'd be all for it. They know that.

"Okay. Two hours. That'll give the horses some time to relax. Gryphon, is there a village nearby where we might be able to shelter from the storm? I don't think we'll stay dry for much longer."

"I'm not sure, but the sign would suggest that there's a settlement nearby. How about we continue slowly along the road and Lennox can catch up?"

"Alright. Lennox, you'll be able to track us should we find a shelter. If not, howl. I do love your howl."

My wolf winks at me. "I'll howl for you any day."

Gryphon was right, the sign was indeed close to a village. It's only ten houses along the road, including one sorry looking pub. We're far away from Parseldon to dare to go in there. We've not seen any traces of pursuers and Gryphon would know if any sirens lived here. It's very handy that he had to learn all the big siren families by heart, including where they live, when he was a child. It helps us stay clear of certain towns and villages.

The pub is dimly lit and has seen better days. Some tables haven't been cleaned in years, at least that's' what they look like. A barmaid gives us a curious glance but doesn't ask any questions. The menu consists of stew, stew or stew. At least they have a variety of ales and beers on offer, plus an apple juice for Sophie.

While we sit and wait for our food, the rain starts to fall outside. Poor Lennox. This pub may not be the best ever, but at least we're dry and will soon have food in our bellies. We've ordered an extra portion of stew. In theory, it's for Lennox when he joins us, but I'm pretty sure it'll end up in my stomach before then. After all, I'm eating for five.

"Can I try your beer?" Sophie asks and pulls one of the tankards towards herself. Cheeky girl.

"Go ahead. You won't like it."

She gives me a doubtful look and takes a big sip. A white line of foam clings to her upper lip, making me grin. She's adorable.

"You're right," she admits to my surprise. "It tastes like horse piss."

"Language," Gryphon says immediately.

"Horse pee. Better?"

He nods. "Much."

"Why do you drink this stuff when it tastes so bad?"

Ryker laughs. "It's an acquired taste. I think your taste buds change when you become an adult and suddenly you don't mind it anymore."

The barmaid brings our stew in large, earthen bowls. My mouth waters at the sight. Those are portions to make a cat very happy. A few pieces of meat swim in the otherwise watery soup, but I don't care. I shovel it into my mouth, spoonful by spoonful, and am done by the time the others haven't even eaten half of theirs.

Without a word, Ryker pushes the spare bowl towards me. I give him a grateful grin and get going. Some of the meat is dry and chewy, even though it's been cooked in broth. Who cares. It's food.

Even after emptying my second bowl, I'm still hungry. The human female stares at me from behind the bar, clearly shocked at how much I'm eating. I shoot her a grin.

"Could we have two more bowls of stew, please? Maybe some bread, too?"

She nods wordlessly and disappears in the kitchen again.

"I wish they had dessert," Ryker mutters. "That's one of the things I love best about being able to shift. Dessert. Cats only really have a main meal. Well, several meals a day, but no starters or desserts. And treats only if we have humans to give them to us. You don't find them in the wild."

"What was it like being a cat?" Sophie asks. She's not talked to Ryker much, spending most of her time with Gryphon, but she's finally warming up to the other guys.

He shrugs. "Normal. I didn't know anything else. Kat probably told you that I didn't even know I was a shifter until she and her friends told me. Even after I knew I was a shifter, I couldn't shift. Nobody had ever taught me to. It was only when I had no other choice, when I had to save both Kat and my son, that I finally managed to. Ever since, it's been easy."

"Do you still feel more cat than human?"

Ryker nods. "I don't think that's ever going to change. I spent all my life as a cat and you can't just erase that. That doesn't mean that I don't like walking on two legs though. It's a very different world, not just because there's dessert."

Sophie wrinkles her forehead in an adorable frown. "If I'd grown up as a cat, do you think I'd feel the same?"

"I don't think we'll ever know. Do you feel human?" he asks gently.

She shakes her head. "I wasn't allowed to shift very often, but I never felt like the humans working for my parents. They were always very different. They even move differently, as if they have trouble coordinating their limbs."

Ryker chuckles. "That's humans for you. They don't even land on all fours if you throw them."

Gryphon snorts. "I don't do that either. And I'm not human."

"Yeah, but you're human on the outside," Sophie says, rolling her eyes. She's had that argument with him a lot. "All you can do is a bit of mind magic."

"A bit of mind magic?" Gryphon repeats in mock outrage. "I will have you know that I could make that barmaid do a handstand while singing the national anthem."

His eyes widen as soon as he realises his mistake.

Sophie's grin widens. "Do it. I challenge you."

Ryker and I exchange a look. Our siren can't back down now. He wants to impress Sophie, even if that means doing something he'd usually avoid.

Gryphon sighs. "Alright, but I'll make her do something else. To cheer up Kat."

"I don't need cheering up-," I protest, but then shut up. I'm curious what he's about to do. A bit of entertainment can never go amiss.

"Madam?" he calls out and she appears behind the bar. "Could you make us some dessert, please?"

She looks at him in annoyance. "Dessert isn't on the menu."

"That was without my powers," he whispers to Sophie before turning back to the human. "Please make us dessert."

Her eyes turn blank and she nods, rushing to the kitchen.

"Why did you say 'please'?" Sophie asks. "You could have just ordered her to do it."

"Because I like being polite. Just because you can manipulate other people doesn't mean you should do it, or that you have to be evil about it. Manners are important."

She goes quiet as she ponders that. Gryphon grins at Ryker and me with a smug expression.

"You could have specified what dessert," I say just to rile him up.

"I did. Mentally. I didn't want to spoil the surprise."

Oh, I could kiss him. If he wasn't on the other end of the table and next to my little sister, I would. I'll have to do it later instead.

Before dessert arrives, Lennox joins us, completely drenched and looking miserable. I rummage in our bags until I find a blanket for him to use as a towel. He takes it with a grateful smile and starts with his hair. Vain dog.

"Did you find anything?" I ask before he's done. Sue me, I'm both curious and impatient.

"Yes, I did." His voice is grave. This can't be good news. "I found a body. Definitely a shifter. He was old, in his sixties maybe, which makes him the oldest shifter I've ever seen. We rarely survive that long, not in this country."

Ryker slides onto the wooden bench next to me, freeing up a chair for Lennox. "How did he die?"

"His head was smashed in, from behind. It looked like he never had the chance to defend himself. What a cowardly attack. I bet he was a local who knew the person who did that."

"What makes you think he was a local?" I ask.

"He didn't have any bags with him, only a wallet in his pocket. His shoes weren't made for long walks, and there was a slight smell of alcohol on him, as if he'd had a pint or two before walking home. Maybe he was here.

Gryphon, if I ask the owner of the pub, can you make them forget about it after?"

The siren nods. "No problem. But let me ask the questions, that makes it easier."

The waitress chooses that moment to return with a large plate of steaming brownies. Oh my goodness. Chocolate is second only to catnip, especially chocolate that's hot and melty. I grab one of the brownies before she's even set the plate on the table.

Sophie is almost as fast. Just like her big sister, she's got a sweet tooth that she never got to indulge back home. Yet another form of torture her adoptive parents put her through.

"Delicious." I snatch a second one. "I love you, Gryphon."

"Glad to hear it. Just leave one for me and I'll love you too."

"Hey, I very much hope you love me already."

"Ew!" Sophie explains. "Stop it."

I give her a wide, chocolatey grin. "Want me to kiss him to prove how much I love him?"

She covers her face with her hands. "Ew. No. Get a room."

Ryker laughs. "Maybe we should do that. The rain seems to be getting worse. If this pub has a room for us, let's take it. Hopefully, it'll have cleared up by morning."

"Madam, do you have two rooms for us?" Gryphon calls. He must be using his powers for the woman doesn't blink an eyelid at him only asking for two rooms despite there being five of us.

"Of course, I'll make them up right away. How many beds do you require in each?"

The siren wiggles his eyebrows at me. "Four in one of them, and please push them close to each other. If there's no room for that, two or three next to each other are fine too. We're happy to share."

I mentally rub my hands. Finally, I'll get some me-time with the guys again. Without Sophie in the same room. I love this pub.

CHAPTER TWENTY-TWO

Being snug and warm under a thick blanket while the rain prattles onto the roof above you must be one of the most comforting feelings out there. And having two warm, male bodies on either side of you is even better.

Lennox is still downstairs, using the pub's phone to call Mr Moon. Hopefully, his former boss and alpha werewolf will be able to send some people here to investigate the killing. We really don't have the time, as bad as I feel about it. A kick against my solar plexus reinforces that. I wince before I can stop myself.

These abominations inside me always seem to get more active in the evening, especially once I lie down.

"Are they kicking again?" Gryphon asks and snuggles closer to me.

"Yeah. I wish they'd just sleep."

"I could try and use my powers on them. I've never tried doing that on babies that are still in the womb, but who knows. It definitely works on babies outside. My mother always calmed my sister that way. She couldn't stand it when either of us cried."

Darkness rolls over his gaze and I reach out to him, cupping his face and pulling him close until I can kiss him. He doesn't need another invitation. He ravishes me, kissing me hard and passionate.

"Hey, don't forget about me," Ryker complains and sits up. "I thought we were going to wait for Lennox."

We ignore him. Gryphon slides a hand under my top and cups my breast. My boobs are incredibly sensitive right now and I think they've increased in size. Yet another thing to hate about this whole situation. When I sneak over rooftops and jump from house to house, I can't have bouncy boobs get in the way. I guess I won't be doing any sneaking until after I'm relieved of my parasites. With how much I must weigh, I'd probably crash through any roof I'd try to stand on.

I hate being pregnant so much.

Ryker sighs and pulls back the blanket, exposing my body.

"I see you've started without me," he says and cups my other breast, gently massaging the nipple.

I moan against Gryphon's mouth and almost bite his tongue. He seems to take that as the signal to become a little rougher and nips my bottom lip. I flash my teeth push him back onto the mattress. I can't move as fast as I like, but I'm still on top of him quicker than he can react. I bend his head to one side and sink my teeth into the nape of his neck. Blood fills my mouth.

Oh. My. Goodness.

So sweet.

"Kat, what are you doing?" Ryker asks, sounding very confused. "Are you going feral again?"

I lick my lips, enjoying the tangy taste of Gryphon's blood. "Just having a second dessert."

Gryphon stares up at me, his eyes wide, but he doesn't

try to get away from me. He just seems confounded at what I'm doing. I've nipped him before, and he's returned the favour, but I've never bitten him to lick his blood. That's new. And kind of scary.

I reach for my cat, but she's mostly part of me again. We're no longer as separate as we were when the guys found me. There's no danger of me going feral and losing myself.

"You taste good," I mutter and lick his wound again. My teeth have left deep indentations on his skin; this might scar. A permanent mark on him. It totally turns me on. I've marked him as mine.

"Hormones?" Ryker suggests weakly. "I've heard they can mess with a woman's mind."

I hiss at him. "I don't have hormones."

"You most certainly do. I've heard of human females craving weird things like pickles with ice cream or fish fingers with custard when they're pregnant. Maybe you're in the same position, except that you're hungry for siren blood rather than ice cream?"

I take a moment to think. "No, I also crave ice cream. It's just that he is here and ice cream isn't. Will you stop interrupting us?"

"Kat, could you be having vampires?" Gryphon asks, his eyes still wide with confusion. "That might be the cause."

"Vampires don't exist."

"Actually, they do, but not as they are in the folk tales. They're distant relations of succubi, but instead of feeding off sexual energy, they need life energy to survive. Blood is the most common way to get that, but they can also find it in other sources. It's just that drinking blood is so unusual that it's become attached to vampires in stories."

I exchange a look with Ryker. "Did you know that?"

"Know what?" Lennox asks and enters the room. He stops to stare at my bloody chin and the bite marks on Gryphon's chest, but quickly covers his surprise.

"That vampires exist," I tell him.

"No, I didn't. And I don't believe it. Not after travelling the country for months. I've met a lot of weird and freaky beings, but not a single vampire."

"They're real," Gryphon insists. "I've met some at one of my father's parties. They look perfectly human from the outside. I don't know if they have a particular smell to you shifters, but the only way I can identify them is because my powers don't work on them. Not even a tiny bit. They have an intrinsic mental shield that's impossible to break. Other kinds of supernaturals are harder to influence and it often fails, but it's not completely impossible like with vampires."

"Why are we talking about vampires?" Lennox asks and takes off his shirt. For a moment, I'm distracted by the sight. I lick my lips. I want to mark him too, and then Ryker. Feed off them, drink their blood, become one with them.

One of the babies kicks me again.

I startle. I called it a baby. Not a parasite. Okay then, something's definitely wrong with me. The blood-drinking was a little weird, but this just takes the biscuit.

"Kat drank my blood so now we think she might be carrying vampires," Gryphon summarises with a wry smile.

"Ah. I see. Gryphon, can you somehow use your mind magic thingy to find out?"

Which brings us back to the original question. I frown. Do I want Gryphon to manipulate my offspring?

There you go, that's a more neutral word. Not as negative as parasites but also not as emotional as babies or kittens.

"Don't make them do anything weird," I warn him. "Just check if they're vampires and maybe give them a little encouragement to stop kicking me."

One of them punches me hard for emphasis. I gasp. They're getting stronger by the hour. I'm not sure what Delaney did to them, but they're growing much faster than even shifters should. I'm starting to doubt that I'll get to three months at the rate they're developing. I'd be a walking planet by then.

"I'll have to sit up for that."

It takes me a moment to realise that I'm sitting on Gryphon's chest. I give his wound one final lick - yum - before climbing off him. It may have been more of a roll. Is this how sea lions feel?

Gryphon places both hands on my bump and closes his eyes. Silence falls as we all watch him. I wish I had his powers. I want to be able to feel my offspring's mind too. Just to make sure they're not mutants, animals or otherwise corrupted. It would give me a lot of peace of mind to know that I'm not carrying monsters.

"I can reach all of their minds," Gryphon mutters, deep in concentration.

Phew. No vampires. That's a relief already. I would have had no idea what to do with them. Would they have drunk my blood rather than my milk? I don't even want to know.

"You were right, Ryker, two of them are unquestionably cat shifters. They've got the same mental signature as you two."

Kittens? I'm really going to have kittens?

A strange warmth spreads within me. Tiny, mewling, adorable kittens. Pouncing around, not quite steady on their feet, tumbling and rolling, and those cute little mini meows...

"I've got hormones," I tell the guys. "I feel them, right now. Get them out of me."

Ryker snorts. "I think that's not quite possible. Why, are you having strange cravings?"

"Besides siren blood," Lennox quips with a lopsided smile.

I don't explain; I wouldn't know what to say. I don't want to admit that I'm all gooey about kittens.

"Two kittens," Gryphon repeats. "And two sirens. But they're not just sirens. I think they may have shifter blood too. There's something un-siren about them."

"Un-siren?" I echo, all the warmth disappearing as reality comes crashing in. "In a good or bad way?"

Gryphon opens his eyes and sits back, removing his hands from the bump. I pull the shirt down again to hide that unsightly swelling. "One of them reminds me of Lennox, but where would werewolf genes come from? And the other one is neither cat nor wolf, something I've not come across before. But remember, this is all just speculation. I've never tried this with unborn babies before."

"If that Delaney arsehole is the father, there can't be any wolf DNA," Lennox says with a growl. "And I doubt your body managed to hold onto my seed for months before fertilising it."

"Seed." Ryker makes a vomiting noise. "What an ugly word."

"He calls himself Sophie's father even though he isn't," Gryphon muses. "And we're only going on what Sophie said. She may have misunderstood. Or he meant he's the father as in the creator rather than the sperm donor. Maybe they're clones. Or he added shifter DNA from a gene bank."

"There's no shifter gene bank," Lennox says, rolling his

eyes. Maybe there's one for you posh sirens, but most of us aren't rich or even desired enough to have such a thing. Remember the shifter children back home, when we tried to find the ones who'd eaten the poisoned sweets? Most parents were embarrassed to have half-shifter bastards."

He may have taken a random werewolf's sperm and put it inside me. I shudder. It may be better than having been raped by Delaney, but it's still not exactly what I could feel comfortable with. I still don't know why he even did this. We destroyed the Pack's labs and facilities, but I'm sure they weren't the only ones who know how to clone someone. He wouldn't need me for that. No, I think I'm beginning to understand. He didn't want clones, pure replicas of something that already exists. He tried changing Sophie, gave her a metal eye, attempted to turn her cruel by giving her the power to hurt others. It didn't work. Now, he's trying to make his own creations, using me as his template. He's had years to study Sophie. From what she's said, he's experimented on her ever since she was born.

That's one half of the genetic material completely understood and researched. The other half is the unknown. I doubt he'd introduce something random. This must be samples that have also been studied. Maybe there are other clones out there, wolf clones, and he's made a kitten-pup in a lab.

Again, I shudder. There are too many variables, but I think I'm right. No, I'm convinced of it. That's what he did. It fits. Making something he can call his creation. If I hadn't escaped, he would have been able to study the babies from the moment they were born.

I wonder if the two kittens are my clones or if he used another cat shifter's genes.

And the fourth, a different shifter. Most shifters are

werewolves; others are rare. It's why I'd never met another cat shifter before Ryker. I don't even know what others are out there. Please don't let it be a cow shifter. I've got a thing about hooves, I've noticed that during the last few days while on horseback. They creep me out. Not having toes is just weird.

"Are there cow shifters?" I ask the guys.

Gryphon clears his throat. "What?"

"Cow shifters. You know, cows that shift to human form."

"I've never heard of them," he says hesitantly. "Why?"

I clutch my bump. "Because one of them might be inside me."

Suddenly, tears are streaming down my face. I try to stop them, but they've turned into a salty waterfall.

The guys crowd around me, hugging me from all sides, while I break into sobs.

"I've got hormones," I sniffle, "and I hate them."

CHAPTER TWENTY-THREE

We never end up having sex. Instead, we speculate most of the night about what kind of shifters may be growing inside of me. By the time the first sun rays break through the waning storm clouds, I'm no longer feeling as creeped out. Parasites have become offspring and almost babies. Whether that's due to hormones or the fact that I finally know that there are no emotionless grunts growing within me, no idea. Not that I care.

"I want waffles," I tell the guys as soon as the craving pops into my head.

"Not sure they have those here," Gryphon yawns. "But I can try and get the barmaid to make some. And then we should leave before the weather turns bad again. I want us to put some distance between us and this weird place where they kill shifters."

I couldn't agree more. I stretch and get out of bed, taking off my clothes to change. Fuck. It's grown yet again. How does this even work? I'm eating a lot, but not this much.

Lennox wolf whistles. "You're beautiful."

"Do you ever feel like you're about to topple forward?" Ryker asks with genuine curiosity. "You look like it."

I shoot him a glare. "I'm massive but I can still stand on two feet without falling over, thank you very much. Can I get some clothes from one of you? I doubt I'll fit into my own, not with this." I point at my bump with disgust. Just because I'm slowly getting used to the idea of having a litter doesn't mean I like the changes my body is undergoing.

Lennox nods and hands me a shirt and trousers. I need a belt for those but they're a lot more comfortable than what I wore yesterday. If I continue to grow at this rate, I'll need to resort to dresses soon.

"Kat!"

Sophie's cry makes me whirl around. It's not come from the room next door, but from downstairs, the pub. What the hell is she doing there?

I run as fast as I can with my bump and giant boobs, storming down the stairs. My knives are still in the bedroom, but if necessary I can partially shift to use my claws.

Anger races through me when I take in the scene in the main room of the pub. Four burly men surrounding Sophie, with one of them pressing a bread knife against her throat. His hand is shaking slightly; I doubt he's ever killed anyone before. That will make things easier. He won't cut her just yet.

The barmaid from last night stands a little apart from them, but she's gloating and looking very pleased with herself. Guess Gryphon's spell has worn down.

"Get out of here," one of the men tells me not unkindly. "We don't hurt pregnant women."

I raise an eyebrow. "But you hurt children?"

He scoffs and spits on the floor. The barmaid winces

audibly but doesn't say anything. "This isn't a child. She's a changeling. Martha told us. Now go before I change my mind."

While he's been talking, the guys have taken their positions. The humans don't know it yet, but Ryker is waiting outside the front door, ready to storm in and take them from behind by surprise, while Lennox and Gryphon are at the top of the stairs, hidden in the shadows. I bet Gryphon has some poison darts and blades ready to throw.

Sophie has figured it out too. A small smile plays around her lips, despite the knife at her throat.

"What's a changeling?" I ask innocently.

"A fairy child exchanged for the real babe," one of the other men says, one with a long beard that looks like it houses several generations of lice. "We usually catch them before they grow up, but we're not afraid to deal with them once they're this age. This isn't a real child."

Sophie flinches at the words. I'm going to have to talk to her later and explain how these humans are deluded and completely wrong.

"Is that why you killed the old man?" I ask. "We found a body nearby."

The first man nods grimly. "Aye, that's Toby. Would never have expected him to be anything like that, but Fib watched him turn into a wolf last full moon. It brings shame on all of us. We should have known."

The disgust on their faces makes me tremble with anger. So much ignorance, so much hate.

"He wasn't a changeling," I snarl, my voice dripping with poison. I wish I had my weapons to hurt them just like they hurt their fellow villager. "Not born of fairies. He was a shifter, a werewolf. And if you didn't notice that before, I assume that none of your livestock ever went missing, which means that he refrained from giving in to his wolf nature. You should have been proud of him, praised him. Not killed him."

None of the men look guilty in the slightest. That seals their fate.

I exchange a look with Sophie. She's ready. So am I. My muscles are strung to jump. I just hope the bump won't get in the way.

"Now!" I shout and everything happens at once.

Sophie kicks the man holding her into the balls while twisting out of the blade's way. The smell of blood permeates the air, but it's only a small scratch on her throat; it'll heal within minutes.

I land on beard-guy, toppling him over. I adjust myself so that I sit on his pelvis, pinning him to the ground. At the same time, the door crashes open and Ryker storms into the room. Gryphon and Lennox have already joined the fray. They deal with the other men, while I grin at my victim and let claws sprout from my fingers. His eyes widen in fear and hate.

"You're one of them," he hisses.

"Didn't Martha tell you? We all are."

And then I cut his throat. My claws slice through his skin like butter. They're made for killing. I may not be a changeling sent to Earth by fairies, but I'm a shifter and I'm proud of it.

He gurgles and grasps his throat. He seems surprised at the turn of events. Guess he didn't expect to die today. Just before he dies, he kicks his legs, not very strongly but it's enough to bring me off balance. I fall forward, on top of him, squeezing my bump uncomfortably.

Pain shoots through my belly. Fuck. Then his blood touches my lips and I forget about the pain. I greedily lap up the blood pouring from his opened throat.

"Kat," Ryker groans. "Not again."

Another sharp pain in my insides rips me from the soothing feeling the blood has given me.

"Ouch."

"What's wrong?" Gryphon asks, by my side in an instant. "Is it the babies?"

He helps me up, leading me away from the dead human and onto a chair. I suddenly feel very pregnant and very vulnerable.

"It's okay, no worse than their kicks," I pant. "Just give me a moment."

Ryker comes over with a wet cloth and wipes my face. I guess he doesn't like seeing me covered in blood, even though it's not my own and it's delicious.

I search the room to distract me from the pain. "Sophie, you alright?"

My little sister smiles and climbs on the chair next to me. "It was a little scary, but we showed those arseholes."

"Language," Gryphon says automatically.

"Nice kick you gave him," I praise her and wince again as more pain shoots through my abdomen. Did someone give my babies knives to poke me from the inside? Or are they trying out their claws? Either way, I need them to stop.

"Where's the pain?" the siren asks gently and lifts my shirt. I let him. It's not like I can stop him in my current state.

"Everywhere. Point at a place and it'll be one that hurts. I think they're throwing a party in there."

"It was silly of you to fight. You should have let us handle it."

I glare at him. "No way. You don't know me very well if you think I could stand back and let you have all the fun."

He sighs. "I know. It's just wishful thinking. You need to

take care of yourself. You're not as agile and invincible as you usually are. It's already risky to have you ride on a horse at this state of pregnancy."

I gulp at the thought of sitting on a horse. No way.

"I think I'll walk today," I mutter.

The guys look at me with pity. I growl at them. I don't want their pity. It's not like that's going to make it any better.

"Maybe we can find you a cart," Lennox suggests. "Those humans look like farmers. I'm sure one of them has a cart at home that we can borrow."

"Steal," Sophie corrects. "Stealing isn't nice. It's against the rules."

"So is trying to kill little girls," Ryker replies darkly. "We're only taking what we're owed for this inconvenience."

Inconvenience. I wince again. Yes, those miniature shifters must have claws. Or something worse is going on.

"Gryphon, what do contractions feel like?" I ask as innocently as I can.

He sucks in a breath. "Do you think you're having contractions? It's too early. You're big but not big enough for four babies."

"Just in theory."

"Ehm, I have no idea. It's not like I've ever had any myself. At university, they said a dull ache in your lower back and abdomen. Does it feel like you need to push?"

I shake my head. "No, thank goodness. And the pain is sharp, definitely not dull. I'd love to have dull pain instead."

Gryphon runs upstairs and returns with his stethoscope. Not that he'll hear more with that than I can already. The four heartbeats haven't changed. I don't think any of my babies are in distress.

He tells me exactly that. "They sound normal. Let's stay here for a bit longer until your pain subsides. Guys, let's make her some food."

"I knew you shouldn't have knocked out the barmaid," Lennox complains and points at the unconscious woman on the floor. "I have no idea how to make waffles."

I chuckle despite the pain. "I'm no longer craving them. Now I'm in the mood for raw, bloody meat. Might be a side effect of the fight though. I don't suppose I can persuade you to bottle some of the humans' blood for me?"

Lennox looks at me with a quizzical expression as if he's trying to figure out if I'm joking or not. I'm not quite sure myself. I want more blood, but I also feel disgusted by that desire.

"I'll find a cart," the wolf says. "Ryker can make breakfast."

He's out of the inn before any of us can stop him. I sigh. I don't need a cart. As soon as the pain stops, I'll be able to get back on a horse. It won't be comfortable, but I'll suck it up and won't complain. I've been through worse. This isn't a permanent state. Soon, I'll push out those babies and everything will be back to normal, with the exception that we'll have to deal with four tiny shifters. I think we'll need a nanny. Maybe we can find a local shifter who's experienced with kittens and pups. And a calf, in the worst-case scenario.

Ryker disappears into the kitchen while Gryphon stays with me, listening to my belly with his stethoscope as if that's going to make things better. Sophie shifts around on her chair, clearly bored.

"Have you packed your things yet? And you could check on the horses."

She jumps up, excited at the prospect of getting to spend time with her beloved Kidril. If we're going to keep that horse, we'll have to get a stable. There won't be space next to our house, so we'll have to find an alternative location. I'll let Benjamin deal with that; he's great at logistics.

Suddenly, something wet touches my thighs. I shriek and look between my legs, expecting blood. It would match the pain. But no, it looks like I've peed myself.

"Gryphon..."

He follows my gaze and gasps.

"No, not yet. Not here. Not now. No, please not."

He's talking nonsense, stammering like an idiot.

"What's happening," Sophie asks with innocent curiosity. "Did the babies make you pee?"

"Her waters have broken," Gryphon replies tonelessly. He runs his hands through his long hair, looking helpless and confused. That's not exactly confidence-inspiring. He's supposed to be the one who knows what's happening. He's the doctor. Almost.

It takes a moment for his words to register. My waters have broken. Oh my goodness.

"Does that mean I'm having the babies?!"

I scream rather than ask. I think I'm becoming hysterical. The pain plus my soaked trousers plus the taste of human blood still in my mouth is messing with my brain.

"Yes, you'll be going into labour," he says. He sounds like he's run several miles. "We need to get ready. Even if your labour takes long, and it often does when it's your first time, we'll never make it to Attenburgh. But it's too soon, we don't know how developed the babies are, if they can breathe on their own. We need medical supplies, I can't do this on my own, and you're in pain, this isn't how it's supposed to be, and..."

He trails off, his eyes wide with panic. While my own emotions are quickly turning mute, he's about to go crazy.

"I'll get Lennox," Sophie volunteers. She's amazingly calm as she walks rather than runs out of the pub.

Ryker isn't. He's in the doorway leading to the kitchen, staring at me open-mouthed, clinging to the door handle for dear life.

"Kittens?" he asks.

I shrug. "Looks like it."

All my hysteria has gone. I'm dead calm. Dead inside. I think this is the only way I'm able to function. This is where all my assassin training comes in. Stand back, look at the situation, avoid any emotional attachment. Use your brain rather than your heart. Don't judge, analyse. What's the next step? What do we need to do to survive?

"Towels," Gryphon mutters. "A pub like this should have lots of towels. And warm water. Bandages if there's bleeding. Blankets to wrap the babies in once they're born. A knife for the umbilical cords. What else? What am I forgetting?"

I leave him to it. The pain is finally getting less and I really want to get out of my soiled clothes.

"Ryker, can you get me another pair of trousers? And panties?"

My wolf stares at me for a moment, dazed and confused, then nods and disappears up the stairs.

"Towels, towels, towels."

Gryphon recites it like a mantra and begins to rummage through the cupboards behind the bar. I let him do whatever he needs to cope. I've never seen him this flustered before. It feels strange and I kind of want to hug him and tell him everything is going to be okay. But I'm not sure he'd want that. And it would be a lie. I don't have any idea if things will turn out alright. Everything seems to be stacked against us.

"Help!" Sophie suddenly shouts from outside, echoing her earlier cry for help.

Please, not again. What is destiny throwing at us now?

"Kat, stay here," Gryphon orders just as Ryker comes running.

"What's happening?"

I push myself to my feet and take a few experimental steps. The pain is still there but it's turning from stabbing to something deeper, not quite as intense.

I turn to them both. "Let's find out. Got any weapons?"

"You're staying here," Ryker commands.

"Help!"

There's no way I'm not running to my sister's aid. I ignore the guys and run - it's more like a fast waddle - outside the pub. Bright sunlight hits my eyes and I blink, momentarily blinded. Several figures surround the building; at least fifteen of them.

Their scent hits me. Mutants. They've found us. And among their stink is the smell of Lennox's blood. I search for him, but neither Sophie nor Lennox are anywhere to be seen.

Ryker and Gryphon join me, pressing close against my sides. The siren slips two knives into my hands. I grip them tight, immediately feeling stronger. This is going to be a fight just like any other.

One man steps forward, taller than most of the grunts. I recognise him immediately despite the sunlight making it hard to see his features properly. Lord Delaney. He's here.

"And so we meet again."

His voice is just as cold and emotionless as I remember. Even his posture is the same as back in Attenburgh when I first saw him. Arrogance leaks from his pores. He thinks he has won and he's enjoying it.

"I have come to collect my creations," he says and stares at my large belly. It's not just curiosity; there's something like desire in his icy eyes. He appraises me from top to bottom like an object he's about to buy. I'm sure that's all I am to his eyes. A commodity he can use in his experiments. He doesn't see me as a person and I bet he doesn't think that about Sophie either. Poor girl, growing up in this man's household. It's a miracle she's the child she is today.

"If you go now, I might let you live," I reply just as calmly. "There is nothing for you here."

He flashes his teeth in the most humourless grin I've ever seen. "You're mistaken, my dear. Once I've killed your companions, I'm going to watch you give birth to my creations. Then I'll kill you myself, for all the trouble you've given me. I'd planned to let you live so that you could bear me another set of test subjects in the future, but I think that would be too much effort. You've proven I can't trust you."

I can't help but laugh. "Why on Earth would you trust me?"

He seems confused by the question but doesn't reply. Instead, he turns to his goons. "Make sure she stays alive."

They nod and salute as one. Creepy. They're like robots, unlike the two mutants who attacked us near the bridge. Those almost had a sense of humour, while these have lost all their humanity.

I swirl the knives around, getting a feel for them. One of them is one of my own, while the other is heavier and might belong to Gryphon. I'm going to take great pleasure in slicing open Delaney's stomach. Then I'm going to feed him his innards. I smile in anticipation. A good fight is just what the doctor ordered.

"Kat, can you hear me?"

Lennox's whisper is almost inaudible. Thank the Catnip Gods, he's nearby. I watch the grunts closely, but they don't react. Hopefully, their hearing isn't as good as mine. Ryker places his hand on my lower back, signalling that he's listening too.

"They knocked me out and have me tied up in the cottage with the red roof down the road. Sophie managed to get away from them, but I'm not sure where she is now. I'm about to shift, but I'm not sure that'll be enough to get free."

Anger rises in me. They hurt my Lennox. Yet another reason to give them a whole world of pain.

"Would you like to give yourself up freely?" Delaney asks with a cold smile. "Like last time? I have to say, I enjoyed that moment immensely. That look of absolute devastation. The way your confidence disappeared within a single moment. Beautiful."

I want to puke. It sounds like he jerks off to the memory.

"No, but feel free to lay down your weapons," I invite him. "I have no intentions of sparing you, but I might kill you quicker."

He scoffs. "You're in no position to kill anyone, girl. Have you looked at yourself in the mirror? You're huge."

Thanks to him. I finally want to get this battle started, but I also want to give Lennox more time to get free. Time to stall a little more.

"Yes, I'm huge. What did you put inside me?"

"This and that. It's just a test if it's possible. You're the oldest, so it made sense to start with you, but of course, the other clones will be next. My people are searching for them as we speak. K.C. is a little young but as soon as she's able to bear children, I have plans for her."

"You want to get your own daughter pregnant?"

He laughs with all the emotion of an iceberg. "She's not my daughter. She's an experiment, just like you and the creations growing inside of you. Having her grow up in the same house as I gave me the opportunity for more intense study. I read all the notes on your development, but I didn't appreciate the freedom you were given, so I had to repeat the experiment with a more controlled environment."

I hope Sophie isn't listening to this. This might break her. She's not very attached to her adoptive parents, but hearing that the man she calls father considers her to be nothing more than a creature to study could destroy her. Gryphon growls. He's just as furious as I am. I won't be able to hold back for much longer.

"Give yourself up," Delaney repeats. "You've never been weaker. You can't win."

I consider that statement, then smile. He couldn't be more wrong. I'm stronger than ever. Yes, I may be hindered by my bump and my pain, but I have the best reason to fight. It's no longer just my life I have to protect. Four tiny beings are inside of me that can't defend themselves. Plus, my sister and my men. We're all in this together. And I'm going to keep us alive no matter what. This torturous leech of a man will not succeed.

I raise my knives, ready to throw them at Delaney. "Come and get me."

That's when the first contraction hits me. My knees give out and my spine catches fire, the pain even worse than before.

One of the knives slips from my hand and lands on the ground with a sad plonk.

We're so fucked.

✿ ✿ ✿ ✿ ✿ ✿

The End

✿ ✿ ✿ ✿ ✿ ✿

Meow! The story concludes in Roar, the seventh and final book in the series. To get updates about the Catnip Assassins and other books, subscribe to my newsletter.

If you want to know how the sirens came to be, take a look at Song of Souls, a standalone m/f romance set in the same world, but several centuries before Kat was even born.

Kat would also like to encourage you to leave a review. Don't tempt her to sharpen her knives. She's scary that way.

AUTHOR'S NOTE

Dear readers,

This book took ages to write, much longer than any of the other Catnip books, mostly because the world suddenly changed. If you're reading this in the far future, you may dimly remember the 2020 lockdown. I hope you future readers are all safe and sound and without this virus that stopped the planet in its tracks.

I'd started Claw just before the lockdown and had planned to let Kat escape soon. Well, suddenly everything changed and now I too was trapped at home, alone, without toilet paper and no longer able to go to my writing café. It didn't just have an impact on my writing, it also changed the story. Kat refused to be rescued. She also refused to escape. Pretty much every single thing you read in this book was unplanned, including the surprise pregnancy. No, I'm not pregnant so that was not related, but I did adopt a new cat during the lockdown.

In May, my bunny Darwin who'd lived with me for six wonderful years died. No other bunny could ever have filled the massive hole he left, so I adopted a rescue cat whose owner had got Covid-19. Sootie spent the first few days hiding in my fireplace (hence the name) but has since turned into a great inspiration for Kat's antics. Sootie has the same black fur as Kat and very sharp claws, but she's absolutely tiny despite being fully grown. Still, her personality is huge and she immediately changed the dynamic of the MacKinnon household – and finally gave Kat the motivation to befriend Sophie and escape.

At the time of writing, the lockdown here in Scotland is slowly easing, but it'll still be months until the schools reopen and I'm not sure yet whether my writing café even survived. I promise you that I won't get Kat anywhere near a kidnapping opportunity, just in case there will be a second coronavirus wave.

Just like all the Catnip books, Claw has been influenced by you, my readers, which involved everything from cat pictures to mouse drawings to discussing why a horse may be called Knickerbocker. Remember the moment Kat thinks about what her vagina will look like after giving birth? I had a very fun discussion about that in my Facebook group, where answers ranged from 'roast beef' to 'loosey-goosey and kinda gooey'. Interacting with my readers is one of the things I love about being an author, so if you're not yet in my Facebook group, search for 'Skye's Book Harem'.

Thank you to everyone who's read this series from beginning to (almost) end. Thank you to my former PA Renée and my new PA Tricia. Thank you to all my friends and family who made the lockdown a little easier with random gifts and dried mango.

Take care and see you in Roar,

Skye

ABOUT THE AUTHOR

Skye MacKinnon is a USA Today & International Bestselling Author whose books are filled with strong heroines who don't have to choose.

She embraces her Scottishness with fantastical Scottish settings and a dash of mythology, no matter if she's writing about Celtic gods, cat shifters, or the streets of Edinburgh.

When she's not typing away at her favourite cafe, Skye loves dried mango, as much exotic tea as she can squeeze into her cupboards, and being covered in pet hair by her bunny diva and her cat princess.

Subscribe to her newsletter:skyemackinnon.com/newsletter

facebook.com/skyemackinnonauthor

twitter.com/skye_mackinnon

instagram.com/skyemackinnonauthor

bookbub.com/authors/skye-mackinnon

goodreads.com/SkyeMacKinnon

patreon.com/skyemackinnon

www.ingramcontent.com/pod-product-compliance
Lightning Source LLC
Chambersburg PA
CBHW030631190726
48286CB00008B/2481